V. J. BANIS

THE
MISTRESS
OF EVIL

Complete and Unabridged

LINFORD
Leicester

First published in Great Britain

First Linford Edition
published 2018

A catalogue record for this book is available
from the British Library.

ISBN 978–1–4448–3698–1

Published by
F. A. Thorpe (Publishing)
Anstey, Leicestershire

Set by Words & Graphics Ltd.
Anstey, Leicestershire
Printed and bound in Great Britain by
T. J. International Ltd., Padstow, Cornwall

This book is printed on acid-free paper

Preface

The castle stood high in the mountains, over a rocky gorge. Many people had lived within its walls, and many had died. No one would live in it now. For a century or more it had remained empty and apart, and in all the world not a living soul cared if it stood or fell.

Not a living soul . . .

1

Victoria Hamilton's Diary

October 3rd, 1973

Today we have begun the last leg in what has been an incredibly long journey. Nearly three thousand miles from the west coast to New York, that far again over the ocean, and a thousand miles across the continent of Europe to get to Budapest — and still a long trip ahead of us before we reach our destination. Notwithstanding my fear of flying, I think if I had it to do over again, I would take John's suggestion and come by plane.

Dear John. Surely the sweetest husband in the world. He looked up just now and saw me writing and said, 'So you were serious about keeping a diary.'

'If you're going to keep one,' I said, 'it seems only right that I keep one too. That way, there'll be two sides to everything.'

He smiled slightly. I think he was

amused at the suggestion that any writing of mine might be scientifically useful. He did not voice this opinion, however, but kept it to himself.

'I have to keep a diary, though I prefer to call it a journal,' he said. 'This trip isn't exactly a pleasure junket.'

'I would agree with that. It has not been a pleasure,' Carolyn said, leaning forward to peer out of the train window. We were creeping through a small railway station, and outside, on the platform, a group of men stared back coldly at the window of our train. 'Look at those men. Talk about dark swarthy types. Are they Slovaks, do you think?'

'Szekelys, perhaps,' John said absentmindedly, giving his attention back to his journal.

'I've never heard of them,' Carolyn said.

'They claim to be descended from Attila and his huns.'

'I shouldn't doubt it,' Carolyn replied. 'Just look at those eyes. They look as if they'd rip us to pieces in a moment. They give me the shivers.'

She clutched her fur about herself as if

she were chilled and gave me a wide grin. Frankly, in my opinion, this trip is little more than a pleasure junket for Carolyn. John had to come for scientific purposes, as he is with the International Geophysical Society. I emphasize that because I am so proud of him. He is only twenty-nine and already he is earning a name for himself in scientific circles. Professor Barton at Tech told me that John is one of the most brilliant people in the study of earthquake phenomena.

I'm ashamed to have to write this, but the truth is, I can't be much more explicit than that about his work or the purpose of our trip. I haven't a scientific mind, and though he's explained it all at length, it is only a muddle to me. It has to do with the causes of earthquakes, which it seems have been linked to movements of underground waters. I.G.S. scientists have been investigating earth movements around the world, and a series of tremors in the Carpathian Mountains brought Romania into the picture.

That is how John happens to be on his way to Romania. And as his wife, I of

5

course felt that my place was with him, although at the moment I think I would rather be back in California, in Los Angeles, in our own little house.

As for Carolyn, my baby sister (I shouldn't call her a baby, really — she resents it as, at twenty, she is only three years younger than I) she felt it would be a lark to come with us and actually see life behind the Iron Curtain.

'You won't see much life where we're going,' John had warned her. 'Except wildlife. The spot we're headed for is a pretty isolated one.'

'I don't care; I shall find it fascinating,' she had insisted, and John had yielded patiently. The agreement between the Society and the Romanian government permitted him to bring his wife and an assistant, and when Carolyn heard this, she quickly declared that she would be his assistant. It means more work for him, of course, since Carolyn will be of absolutely no use in his work; but she wanted to come, and frankly I liked the idea of having her along to keep me company, as John knew. So, Carolyn is with us.

Well, she is enjoying the trip more than I. All day long, while I am impatient at the way we dawdle along, she keeps leaning toward the window, crying, 'Oh, look at that,' and, 'Isn't that remarkable?'

I think she has caught the gypsy spirit of the people we pass in the stations. At least, she is not so fierce-looking as most of them.

October 4th

It seems at times as if this journey will never end. I feel as if I have spent all my life on hard seats in chugging, heaving trains. John has warned us that the place we will be staying at will not be very luxurious. I was hoping, of course, that at the very least we would have hot water. I can think of nothing at the moment more attractive than the prospect of a long soak in a tub.

'The Romanian government is providing us with quarters,' he explained, 'but we'll be out in the mountains, so it's not likely there'll be much choice in accommodations. We'll be lucky, I expect, to get some sort of shepherd's shack.'

I smiled and told him I was sure we would be comfortable. Not wanting to complain, I did not add that I thought a tent and a bed on the ground would seem luxurious after this trip. The train service across western Europe was fine, really, the best I've ever experienced, but in the communist countries there are no first-class trains. Everyone travels the same, which for all practical purposes means that all of the service is slow and all of the equipment is old and in disrepair. Happily, we haven't much longer to bear it.

We spent last night in a town called Klausenburgh. We had decided in advance that the trip was too long and the connections too poor to attempt to make it without a break, so we have been stopping for the nights. What a relief it was to be off those dismal trains, for a few hours at least.

We had a delicious chicken dish for dinner last night, which as I learned from the waiter is called paprika hendle, and is a common dish locally. I hope I can get the recipe while we are in the area. As far as I know, we'll be here for months, so I don't think there is any hurry about such things.

Breakfast was peculiar — peculiar because we three are not used to much more than coffee and toast; but we had learned that the trains did not have dining service and we would probably have to travel all day with no food, so we ate heartily.

The hotel served us stuffed eggplant and something called mamaliga, which was a type of porridge with paprika. Odd dishes for breakfast, but we had also realized that one should not provoke people too much in these countries. Everything had been planned (and paid for, by the Society, happily) in advance; and our duty, as John more than once explained to us, was to go along with the plans without causing problems.

The country through which we are passing is beautiful, in a wild sort of way. We've gone by numerous old castles sitting atop knolls and mountain peaks, looking like something out of Disneyland. There are streams and rivers and rough gorges. The towns are few and small. I begin to see what John meant when he said we would be isolated. We are moving toward a range of distant mountains that John tells me are the Carpathians. That name has an ominous ring, though I can't think why.

The people we see in the towns have dark complexions, with black hair and heavy moustaches — what we would call swarthy. They all look distant, even unfriendly, although some of the women in the last village looked at us with very frank curiosity. I've no doubt they had never seen westerners before.

At every town and station we see men in uniform, reminding us that this is not a free country. There have been frequent checks of our papers and baggage, but as we are traveling under government auspices we are never inconvenienced for long. That is something to be grateful for. On our own, I suspect things would be very much different.

At the last checkpoint, I noticed one of the uniformed men took resentful note of my jewelry and my fur. I feel sure they do not see much of these things here. When he had departed and we were on our way again, I removed all of my jewelry except my wedding ring and put it in the traveling case. I felt safer about it then. I could not put my fur away, though. The weather is decidedly cool and the train car is unheated.

October 6th

How exhausted I am. I can't think how people manage to travel constantly and enjoy it. Of course, they don't spend days in shaky old trains and rattling buses. We are in a bus now, but it's a far cry from what we are used to in the States. This one is so old I wonder how it can get up some of these steep grades. As a matter of fact, it barely does get up some of them, as Carolyn pointed out.

'I could walk up the hill faster than this,' she said to me in a whisper, with a giggle, though I confess I found nothing about our circumstances amusing. 'Not carrying all our luggage,' I said. 'Besides, if you really want to know, John warned me last night that we might end up making part of the journey in a wagon. Transportation is still rather primitive here. Probably we should be grateful for the bus while we still have it.'

We were both whispering because the bus was crowded with locals — those dark-haired, dark-eyed peasants — and we were in the company of a very somber gentleman in military uniform who is to accompany us the rest of the way to our destination. Apparently, government auspices or not, we are not to be trusted traveling here on our own — though for the life of me I cannot imagine what secrets they thought we might discover here. The secret of the back yard privy?

And what a destination! Count Drakul's castle. The idea of our living for some months in a castle is thrilling in itself, but from all I have gathered from bits and pieces of conversation (we're afraid to talk freely in the presence of our personal commissar), this one is out of the ordinary even as castles go.

Well, I've skipped a day in this little book, so I had best fill in that blank. I have a confession which I could not dare tell anyone aloud. I have a purpose in keeping this diary. It is my personal conviction that my husband will someday be famous. It may even be this very journey that will put the seal upon his success.

In that event, every scrap of information about him will be precious. People will want to know as many of the details of his life as they can glean — not only his scientific work, which will be amply recorded in his own journals, but the little personal glimpses that make a biography come to life. A century from now, some eager student may be fascinated to know that paprika has kept my husband awake most of the last few nights. We've had paprika hendle in one form or another every day now, everywhere we have stopped for the night. I don't think I shall bother getting the recipe.

The evening before last we arrived at Bistrita, our last train destination. I suppose that was why we were met there by our military companion, whose name is Skinsky. I rather doubt that spelling is correct, but that's what it sounds like, and he is so unfriendly that I hesitate to ask him for the correct spelling of his name. So, Skinsky he shall remain.

'There is a bus tomorrow for Bukovina,' he explained on our way to the hotel. 'I have reserved passages on it for us. We will leave it at the Borgo Pass.'

He explained all this to John, seemingly assuming that these place names would be significant to him. He was right. John had spent a great deal of time studying maps of the areas, and he seemed to follow this route in his mind with no difficulty.

'Then we'll be right in the Carpathians?' John asked.

Mister Skinsky (Officer Skinsky?) nodded. He was not overly generous with words. Because he seemed disinterested in Carolyn and myself, I had given my attention instead to the village through which we were driving. We were in a taxi, and what a car! To my surprise it was a Ford, but of a vintage much older than I could identify. Prewar, certainly, and showing its age with every rattle and shimmy.

A thought occurred to me just then, and I turned in the seat to ask, 'I suppose there is some sort of house where we are going, or at least rooms for all of us?'

He smiled in what I thought was a patronizing way. 'My government has made available to you Castle Drakul. I think you will find it big enough.'

'Or too big,' John said, frowning. 'I suppose everybody thinks of Americans as wanting the biggest of everything, but a castle is a bit more than we require.'

'There are no other houses where you want to go,' Skinsky said flatly. 'Nor any other accommodations. The area specified in your communications is quite isolated.'

'But if there are people living there . . .'

'The castle is empty. It has been the property of the government for many years. It was available, and by chance was in the exact location that you desired.'

I had already observed that there was no point in arguing anything with our Skinksy. John seemed satisfied with the answer, but I thought Carolyn was not. I had noticed her giving Skinksy a peculiar look when he mentioned our destination. At the next pause in the conversation, she asked, 'What was the name of that castle again?'

He seemed to find her question amusing for reasons I could not understand. 'Castle Drakul. Do you know of it?' he asked.

She gave him a look that I thought was a bit uneasy. Well, of course she would be uneasy. We are all ill at ease, tired and cross. I would be happy to be anywhere just to be done with travel. But a castle — even I have to admit that is rather an exciting thought. Whoever thinks they are going to wind up as guests in a castle?

'I recognize that name,' Carolyn said to him. 'It's been used in books and movies. Not very pleasant ones.'

Something registered in my own mind then. I had been thinking the name was familiar, and suddenly it came to me. 'Drakul? Dracula, of course,' I said. 'All those old monster movies. He was a werewolf, or something like that.'

'A vampire,' Carolyn said.

I could not suppress a shudder, though as a rule I am not susceptible to such fantasy horrors. 'What an odd coincidence,' I said. 'Considering that by either pronunciation the name is so unusual.'

Our companion seemed more amused than ever. He spoke as if addressing a group of not-very-bright children. 'Count Drakul was a Wallachian nobleman of the fifteenth century,' he said. 'A real one, not a make-believe one. He was a great fighter and a hero, a general who led many battles against the Turks. He was also a man whose private appetites were a little strong. It was common with the so-called nobility of that age. This was before the revolution, you understand. The class system that was in place then encouraged a master-slave relationship, which in turn led to many perversities. Drakul was greatly hated and feared by his own people. They called him a monster.

'When a Mister Stoker, who I am told was a writer of sorts, came across the stories of Count Drakul, he took the word 'monster' literally and wrote a book in which he included every sort of myth and fantasy, and in so doing he besmirched a great old name, even though he did change the spelling of the count's name slightly — D-r-a-c-u-l-a.' He paused and looked from Carolyn to me. 'Of course, if these old tales frighten you . . . '

John, who had not seemed to be listening, said at once, 'My assistant and I are scientists, and my wife is not the sort to be frightened by a lot of ghost stories.'

Skinsky nodded, but he gave me a glance that suggested he did not fully believe my husband's evaluation of me. Perhaps he was right and John was mistaken. The idea of a castle haunted by tales of vampires made me nervous for a while, but I have since pushed that thought aside and I am now really looking forward to seeing this castle. Truly I am.

We had come by this time to the hotel at which we were to spend the night. It was a thoroughly charming place, quite old-fashioned — primitive, even; but after the long train trip it was a welcome sight. We were greeted by a cheerful woman in a brightly colored dirndl and a man in shirtsleeves. They were pleased to see us. I suppose there are not many travelers here. We were given clean, comfortable rooms.

Our companion did not share dinner

with us — paprika hendle again under a different name. While we ate, Carolyn brought up the subject of Castle Drakul.

'It's funny, isn't it,' she said, eating the chicken with a gusto I no longer felt it warranted. 'I always thought the Dracula stories were pure fiction. In my wildest dreams, I would never have suspected we'd be going to live in the count's very own castle.'

I was about to reply, but the woman who had greeted us and who also happened to be serving our table chose that very moment to drop a serving dish on the floor. It broke with a loud crash, sending pottery and stewed carrots flying about the room, and there was a general commotion for several moments. Her husband came out, and there was a rapid and excited exchange in a tongue I did not know. I supposed he was scolding her for being so clumsy in front of guests.

There were many furtive glances in our direction. I knew they were discussing us because at one point I distinctly heard her mention the name Drakul. I guessed she was telling him about our eventual destination. I think he told her to be still. Or, to be more specific, to zip up her mouth. That gesture requires little translation. Probably he thought it was neither the time nor the place to discuss our travels. I have observed that the people here are very reluctant to speak their minds.

When later she brought our dessert, a custard dish, I asked if she knew anything about Castle Drakul. When I posed my question to her, she behaved mostly strangely, crossing herself and suddenly insisting that she did not understand English, although she had spoken it rather well up to that point in time.

After she had gone away, I said to John, 'There's something here I don't like. I would swear that woman is frightened at the mere mention of Castle Drakul.'

John gave me an impatient look. Even he was tired from our long trip, and he was a bit irritable. 'You must remember what Skinsky told us — that the count was thought of as a monster around here. Those old stories were no doubt handed down by the peasants to their children, and probably getting well embroidered along the way. By this time his name is probably synonymous with the devil. It's probably how they frighten misbehaving children.' He put down his fork and grew serious. 'Now, Victoria,' he said, 'you're not going to start getting all skittish about this, are you? Because if you are, we'd better start making arrangements right away to send you home.'

I laughed and assured him I was only curious, and I wasn't frightened at all by any ghost stories. He was a bit dubious, but I think I convinced him and the subject was dropped. After that, though, I could hardly tell him that the woman came to see me in the morning before we left to beg me not to continue our trip. Her English was once again fluent and she was really quite frightened. She was actually crying while she pleaded with me.

'Oh, please, dear lady, don't go,' she sobbed, squeezing my hand in hers.

'But I have to go,' I said, trying to be calm in the face of this emotional storm. 'My husband has important work to do and I must be with him.'

'But you don't know what sort of place you are going to.'

I smiled and saw that John had been right. In a place such as this, among a simple and emotional people, the perverse behavior of the old count would have quickly been embroidered with myth and grim fantasy.

When she saw that her entreaties were useless, the kind woman removed from her neck a plain crucifix on a gold chain and insisted upon putting it about my neck. I tried to pay her for the gift, but she would not accept my money. I knew John would say I was being superstitious, but I felt better for having the crucifix and thanked her heartily before we parted.

We left yesterday at midday in, as I have said already, an antiquated bus. Our departure was a bit unusual. A crowd of local people had crowded about the hotel to watch us board the bus. I assumed it was because strangers are infrequent here. When we mounted the rusty steps, the villagers made the sign of the cross and pointed two fingers at us. When we were underway, I asked Skinsky what that gesture meant.

'It is a charm against the evil eye,' he said with a mocking smile. 'These are country peasants. They remain quite superstitious, notwithstanding our modern times.'

I let the subject drop. I do not like the commissar at all. I hope he will not be living with us at the castle. Will they think we need watching? I hope not. Even though I know we will not be hatching any plots against his government, I shall be nervous with someone looking over my shoulder all the time.

Anyway, that was yesterday. Our chuffing bus carried us through the night at its snail's pace, stopping briefly at crude inns along the way for meals and relief. And today is nearly over. It will soon be sundown, and still we creep along. I asked Skinsky several times when we would reach the Borgo Pass, and each time he only told me, 'Soon.'

I hardly slept at all last night, sitting up in a hard seat, bouncing about without cessation. I shall sleep for a week when we reach that castle. I don't care if a legion of werewolves and vampires and the Frankenstein monster himself is roaming the halls.

Well, it is an adventure.

I no longer find the countryside beautiful. I am sick of it.

2

Letter from Miss Carolyn Stuart to Mr. Walter Bradshaw, Los Angeles, California, U.S.A.

October 6th
Darling Walter,
To begin with, you must forgive my writing if it looks a little shaky. We are riding in an absolute Toonerville bus and have been since yesterday noon, going up the most God-awful mountain road I have ever seen. I wouldn't be the slightest bit surprised if any minute now we ran right off the edge of the world and landed on the back of a giant tortoise.

Every bone in my body feels shattered. My stomach is in violent protest against the awful food we have been eating. And poor Victoria looks so absolutely defeated that I have no choice but to try to keep up a brave front. What I wouldn't give to be back in Westwood, having a delicious sundae, and people-watching with you.

Oh, I can just hear you saying, 'You didn't have to go.' And it's true, naturally. But what could I do? I couldn't let Victoria come to the end of the world by herself, and John doesn't count for anything on that score. He gets so wrapped up in his work that he forgets to breathe. And you know what a helpless case Victoria is. Do you know she never learned to drive a car? In Los Angeles. If you can imagine.

But I haven't even told you my really great news. You'll never, ever guess where we are going to be living. I'm not making this up, honest I'm not. We are headed for the castle of Count Drakul, no less. Dracula, in case that spelling throws you off, though that is how they do it here.

It's true. There really was a count, centuries ago. Our guide — the grimmest man I've ever seen — hinted at some dark doings. Something sadistic, I expect, and probably young girls carried off and ravished. Young boys, too, for all I know. And that gave birth to all those ugly legends. Isn't it too much?

Ouch. We just went over a vicious bump. It really has been rough, but not uninteresting. The people are not awfully friendly. The bus is crowded but no one speaks to us, although they are obviously curious, and I often catch them looking at us in what I think writers call a 'guarded' manner.

In the last town, news of our destination got around, and everyone carried on something dreadful, making the sign of the cross and all. Victoria won't admit it, but she's frightened by that sort of thing. She thinks I haven't noticed she's wearing a crucifix, though she never has before. I wonder how she came by it. I would swear she did not own one before this trip.

We're traveling through beautiful country, though, and John amazes me with his knowledge of it. Of course, he's had months to prepare. From Bistrita, where we spent the night (night before last, this is, last night we spent on this infernal bus) we drove through a green sloping land. Forest and hills, that sort of thing. Gabled farmhouses along the road. All very quaint and picture-bookish.

John calls this the Mittel Land and he says the roads have always been kept in poor condition. In olden times, the natives did not repair them because war was always a threat and if the neighboring Turks saw the road being repaired, they would think the locals were preparing for war and so would launch one themselves.

We have begun to drive into the Carpathians. They tower to the right and to the left of us, the sun falling full upon them and bringing out a rainbow of colors — deep blue and purple in the shadows, green and brown in the sun, and all those craggy cliffs leading off into the distance, becoming snowy peaks.

It is spectacular, really. I can't think of anything to liken these mountains to — our Rockies, I suppose, though they are nowhere near so barren as these. From time to time one sees the white gleam of falling water cutting down across the face of the cliffs. Our route up into these mountains is serpentine. We have on three occasions passed horse-drawn carts, and since Bistrita, ours is the only engine-powered vehicle I have seen. That's how primitive it is here. There are many crosses along the roadside. Shrines of some sort, I suppose.

It is nearly night. The light has almost gone, and the mountain peaks are pink with sunset. The people in the bus have begun to stir, as if they expected something to happen soon. Perhaps we are almost there. In any event, I can hardly see to write any more, so I shall close and write again from the castle.

Oh, one more funny thing. A short time back we had to stop because the bus was overheating going up a hill. I thought maybe we'd have to walk a ways, but it seems this is standard procedure; and when the engine had cooled off, we started on our way again.

While we were stopped, I tried to get off the bus to stretch my legs. I don't know what the driver thought I was planning to do, but he nearly had fits. I never did get off the bus, and all our guide would say was that it was forbidden to get out and stroll around where we were. Talk about regulations. Suppose my trip had been necessary?

I can hardly see the paper any more. Bye for now.

Love,
Carolyn

John Hamilton's Journal

October 7th

We are here at last. It has been a grueling trip and Victoria is showing it, though trying hard not to. I suspect I am as well. Carolyn seems bright and fresh as always. She looks so frail, but has incredible strength and self-discipline.

Yesterday we traveled through the Mittel Land. I saw apple trees, plum, pear and cherry, as well as weeping birch, the latter delicate green and silvery-looking without their leaves.

Have seen a few peasants in costumes that date back centuries. Indeed, except for our bus, we seem to have stepped back in time. There is little or no evidence of the twentieth century here. The world has passed this region by. It is a dark place, though, dark and foreboding.

Last evening got very cold. When twilight fell, the shadows appeared to merge with the early snow, creating a contrast of white. As we wound up into the pass, the darkness seemed to close down upon us.

I must guard against becoming fanciful. That way lies folly. There is too much here for the imagination to feed upon.

With night our driver urged the bus on at as fast a pace as it could manage. We rocked about as if on a stormy sea. I knew we were approaching the pass. The people in the bus had become excited. Some were very curious and some looked downright frightened. It is those silly legends about that Wallachian — Drakul, I think his name was. I gather that he was the subject of some books or movies. I never had time for things like that. In fact, they never really interested me much. I was always intrigued by facts, not fantasies.

At last the bus stopped, and Skinsky motioned that it was time for us to get off. The driver kept racing his motor and speaking rapidly in the Romanian tongue. I have given some study to the language, but this was too rapid, and the local accent confused me. The gist of it, so near as I could tell, was that he wanted us to hurry, hurry, hurry. He was most impatient to have us off the bus so he could be on his way. That seems to be universal with bus drivers, but this man behaved as if it were a life and death matter.

He needn't have urged us, however, since we were all as eager to be off that infernal conveyance as he was to be rid of us. It had been an uncomfortable trip, to put it mildly.

I was not surprised to discover a horse cart waiting to take us the rest of the way. We were really and truly quit of the twentieth century now. Carolyn groaned loudly. Victoria looked a bit grim, but she offered no complaint. I patted her hand and told her we hadn't much further to go, although frankly I myself didn't know the exact location of the castle.

It had begun to sleet — a wet, driving rain-snow that chilled us to the bone. The cart was a covered affair probably not unlike those in which our ancestors had crossed the American prairies, with a canvas stretched over its length to shelter us (more or less) from the weather. The driver was a stout mustachioed gentleman who did not seem very pleased to see us. I handed up our luggage and helped the women into the cart, and we were on our way almost at once, Skinsky seated inside with us, while the driver was exposed to the elements — which may have explained his bad temper.

I was facing the rear and could see out, so I kept a fair idea of our travels. I had a glimpse of our bus speeding on its way to Bukovina and I must confess, in the cold darkness, I felt a pang that we were not continuing on with its occupants. But this fancy passed quickly.

We set off at a rapid pace. We talked little. It was difficult to judge time in the dark, tired as we were, but the trip was not a short one. We heard a dog howling somewhere in the distance, and another answering it. I thought that the horses were nervous, but the driver spoke to them in a soothing manner and they went on.

I dozed but woke when Victoria gripped my arm tightly. In the distance there was a strange new sound — a sharper, more eerie howling.

'What on earth is that?' Victoria asked Skinsky, although I already knew what his answer would be.

'Wolves,' he said simply. He tried to look unconcerned, but I had a feeling that was only an act. I did not doze again.

We were in a deep forest now, hemmed in by trees and great towering rocks. The wind rushed down through this narrow pass with a roar, rattling the branches of the trees. Our sleet had turned to snow. We were climbing higher up into the mountains, and the night had grown deathly cold. Victoria huddled closer to me for warmth. The howling of the wolves sounded louder, but I could not say for certain.

From where she sat, Victoria had a view, if a limited one, out the front of our cart. We suddenly came to a halt, and at the same time Victoria again tightened her grip on my arm and gave a little gasp.

'A group of young women,' she said, looking at us with a shocked expression. 'Four or five of them, standing in the road.'

Skinsky had jumped up from his seat and crowded past us to get to the front, so that it was a moment before I could squeeze past Victoria and have a look out the front of the wagon.

When I did, I caught my breath sharply. 'You may be partly right,' I said over my shoulder to my wife. 'Some of these creatures may be females, but I think it an error to call them women.'

'Why, what on earth do you mean?' she asked, unable to see now as I was blocking the view. 'I saw them as plain as day, all in white and not even wearing any coats.'

'We are surrounded by a pack of wolves,' I said as bluntly as I could.

It was quite true. The moon had pierced the dark clouds to reveal a ring of wolves blocking the road and surrounding the wagon. In the silvery light I saw the fierce white teeth and the lolling tongues and the coarse, shaggy hair. There might have been fifteen or twenty of them. They were silent now, staring at us with eyes that looked red in the night, and anything but friendly.

I am no coward, but I do not hesitate to admit that I was struck dumb with fear. Their silence made the beasts more horrible than when I had heard them howling. It was the sort of horror that every man experiences in coming face to face with his worst nightmare.

The silence was suddenly broken. The wolves began to howl, setting up a terrible din. The horses neighed and snorted and reared, torn between their desire for flight and the ring of beasts that encircled us.

Skinsky wore a gun belt, and the driver had produced a rifle from under his seat. Shots rang out. Neither of the men was apparently a very good marksman, for although the wolves were within ten feet of us, not a single one fell.

Nevertheless, the shots produced results. After another grim moment, the wolves turned and disappeared as quickly as they had come, melting into the darkness of the forest. The horses bolted forward with a lurch that threw me back into my seat. We were once again underway. Victoria's eyes were wide with terror. Even Carolyn looked stricken. At that moment, I was too shaken myself to be much comfort to either of them.

We went on even faster than before, climbing, climbing, higher and higher . . . up into those dark, dark mountains.

Suddenly the cart took a fast curve. I had a glimpse of a crumbling stone wall and a gate that hung lopsidedly from a single hinge, and then we were in a courtyard and had come to a stop.

'We are here,' Skinsky said, and I thought even that unfeeling man was glad our trip was ended.

I got out of the cart after him and helped the women down. We were in a courtyard that was partly overgrown with brush, dry and brown now with the winter. We stood before a vast and crumbling edifice. The broken battlements made a jagged silhouette against the moonlit sky. The place looked desolate and forbidding.

We had arrived at the Castle Drakul.

3

Report of Commissar Branislav Skinsky, to Under Secretariat, People's Republic, Council for Economic Assistance, Bukovina, Romania

October 8th

Arrived Castle Drakul 0:20 hours. American scientific party of John Hamilton, assistant Carolyn Stuart, wife Victoria Hamilton, delivered and placed under custody of Citizens Stefen and Olga Petrof. American party all in good health. Have observed nothing of a suspicious nature to date. From all appearances the purpose of their stay — investigation of earthquake causation — appears to be legitimate. Have alerted the Petrofs to be observant. They have issued their assurance that the Secretariat will be advised immediately if anything of a questionable nature arises during the Hamilton party's sojourn.

Written in hand this 8th day of October.
S.B. Skinsky, C.R.A. Victoria

Victoria Hamilton's Diary

October 8th

I'm afraid all my lovely thoughts of staying in a fairybook castle vanished the moment I set eyes on this nightmarish place last night — or, I suppose it was very early this morning. I was sure that once we got here I would fall asleep on my feet, but since we arrived, the dawn is just breaking and I feel wide awake. Perhaps bringing these pages up to date might help make me drowsy enough to fall asleep.

A wolf pack! Imagine! I saw John making entries in his journal, so I am sure he has made mention of our narrow escape from the jaws of the hideous wolf pack. He was so marvelous, so calm and steady. Truthfully, I was sure that both Carolyn and I were going to faint, but I suppose it was fear itself that kept us conscious and alert to the danger.

But the wolves were not half so

frightening as the strange group of women I thought I had seen moments before. John couldn't have seen them, and I surely must not have either. It must have been fatigue and, yes, fear, that made me think they were there — or the shadows of the night were playing tricks on me.

I would have sworn that I saw women, three or four of them, all dressed in white and staring straight at us. The very memory of those eyes makes me shiver still. Could it only have been my imagination? But when John looked — and indeed, when I looked a second time — there were no women, only the wolves surrounding us. Thank heaven the men were armed and could frighten the animals away.

The driver took Skinsky away the moment we disembarked from the covered wagon that brought us here. Actually I feel much like one of those early pioneers, stranded in hostile Indian country.

Skinsky. What a strange man. I'm sure he is convinced that we are some kind of American spy detail sent here to undermine the People's Communist Republic. It could use a bit of undermining, believe me. Everyone is so dour, so poor and impoverished-looking.

Even here at the crumbling castle, the caretaker looks and acts like something right out of an old B-grade movie — very surly, blank expression, cool politeness. His name is Stefen Petrof. I saw him whispering with Skinsky just before Skinsky left us. They all look like Russian agents to me. I can't imagine what they think we might be up to. No one would come here without some major purpose such as John's scientific studies. What would spies want with this place, anyway? Surely there is nothing to spy upon.

I simply cannot believe this castle. It quite scares the wits out of me, but I mustn't let John know that. He'd send me packing in a minute, and I would let him send me off if I didn't want to be with him so desperately. This is the first vacation we've had together in years, if one can call this a vacation. But I just could not face that trip back — not alone, and not yet. I think I will need at least a month to rest up before wanting to tackle that return trip.

A month in this place? Actually, now that I think about it, I don't know which is the worse of two evils: the castle or the trip back to civilization. Skinsky told us that no one has lived in this place for decades, and that is more than obvious. Dust. Cobwebs — oh, one could see that the caretakers had made an effort to make it look presentable to us, but there was only so much they could do with such an enormous place. I think it would take a veritable army to give this place the cleaning it needs.

After Skinsky drove off, we stood in that courtyard, looking up at the frowning walls and blank windows. A great door dominated one wall, and I could see bits of light gleaming through its chinks. We went up a few steps and stood before this immense door while the man, Stefen Petrof, rattled chains and clanked massive bolts and turned rusted keys. The door swung open with a loud, grating sound, moving on hinges that had obviously gone unused for many, many years.

'Just like on *Inner Sanctum*,' Carolyn commented as we went into the castle.

'Don't joke,' I whispered, taking hold of her arm. 'I think it's creepy.'

She giggled. 'Victoria, you'd jump if you saw your own shadow,' she said.

Which just is not true. I'm not the type who frightens easily. Carolyn has always treated me as the helpless sister who needs constant looking after, but in truth I think it's the other way round. I've been protecting her all these years. She thinks she's fooling me, but I have the feeling that my dear little sister is as unnerved by this decaying old relic of a castle as I am.

Once inside, we met another member of the illustrious People's Republic: Stefen Petrof's wife, Olga. Now there's a pair for you. She's just as surly and unfriendly as he is. But at least they both speak English, well enough, anyway, and seem to honestly want to make us comfortable.

My first glimpse of the inside of the castle caused my heart to sink into my shoes. This place hasn't had a good cleaning in centuries, or so it looks. A mammoth staircase started up from a wide stone foyer. Downstairs, cobwebs and debris are everywhere.

I must admit even the Petrofs seem a bit concerned about the untidiness of the place, especially Olga. She apologized time and time again but assured us that the rooms that were prepared for us were comfortable and clean, as indeed they are. She explained that they simply had not had the time to do much with the castle, as they had only been sent up a day or two earlier. Certainly it would take two people a great deal of time to spruce up this old barn, but she promised they would do their best to set things right as quickly as they could.

Our rooms are charming, if you look upon medieval architecture as charming. They are certainly big and spacious, but rather drafty. Furs are everywhere — on the floors, the walls, the beds, the hearths. Fireplaces are in abundance and fires have been lit in some of them, but they don't seem to do much toward cutting the cold unless one snuggles up close to them.

The rooms are lighted by oil lamps. I don't know why I had expected electricity. I suppose I was just being fanciful again. John, of course, being the practical type, knew we would be living without modern conveniences. Never having been in a fifteenth-century (I believe that is the correct time frame) castle, I assumed the conveniences would be primitive, but I never expected them to be this primitive. John merely laughs at me when I frown at the sanitary facilities afforded us. I guess they are laughable, really.

The apartment in which we are housed consists of three large rooms and three smaller ones. The large rooms are bedrooms for Carolyn and John and me, separated by a huge sitting-dining room. The smaller rooms are to accommodate our toilet and closets for storing luggage and equipment.

The sitting room is the nicest of the chambers. It is divided into little sections. It would be a misnomer to refer to the dining area as an alcove because it could well be considered a separate room, it is so large. Off that alcove is the sitting room, with heavy comfortable furniture and roaring fireplaces. Opening off this is a sort of library. The walls are lined floor to ceiling with books, and happily a great many of the books are in English. So at least, in lieu of any other entertainment, I can read to my heart's content.

The table was laid with a very appetizing supper, and after we had refreshed ourselves, we ate heartily of a very sumptuous repast — paprika hendle, of course (which John groaned about) but also two meat dishes that tasted much like veal swimming in a wine sauce and beef simmering in a sauce of sour cream. The food was hot and we all attacked it with gusto. We were half-famished after so long and arduous a trip.

The Petrofs did not stay to serve us. Olga said if we needed them there was a bell cord which we could pull. I wonder where they live. Are their quarters as comfortable as ours? Perhaps not. The locals seem to have a strange fascination with making themselves uncomfortable. From all I have seen thus far of this unusual country, comfort is shunned as if it were a sin. I noticed the looks on their faces when we were traveling. The people looked upon us as though we were idolaters, sinners of the first water.

I see that John has dozed off. The dawn looks so beautiful coming up over the mountains. The gloom of last night is fading already. The sun is bringing another day; and I, like John, am beginning to doze.

Carolyn went to bed a long time ago. Outwardly none of this seems to be bothering her. She was anxious to go off to her own room, almost as if someone were waiting there for her. I suspect she wants to be alone to pour her heart out in another letter to Walter.

I do hope she is planning to marry him. Walter Bradshaw is a very nice man and exactly what Carolyn needs to settle her down. She's gotten a little too headstrong and independent lately — the very model of the modern woman. It's about time she got married. If Walter doesn't settle her down, I am afraid she will wind up being an adventuress. As I thought before, Carolyn has a bit of the gypsy in her.

4

John Hamilton's Journal

October 8th, p.m.

I had one of the best night's sleep in a number of days. Victoria is still sleeping. I assume Carolyn is also. I haven't the least idea of the time, but I see that the Petrofs have cleared away last night's supper and have set out a cold breakfast. Yet the sun is going down, so it is definitely late afternoon or early evening.

This old place is amazing. I can't wait to dig around downstairs and get started with my investigations. I'll need Carolyn's help, though, so I'll have to wait until she and Victoria are up and functioning.

I set to and enjoyed the breakfast (thankfully they don't serve paprika hendle for breakfast) and when I finished, I looked about the apartment.

There are certainly odd deficiencies in the castle. Considering the extraordinary evidence of wealth, I am surprised that the place is in such a state of disrepair. Believe it or not, the table service is solid gold. I hadn't noticed it last night, but then the light was so poor and I was so tired I hardly noticed anything at all.

Imagine eating off solid gold plates. I can't help wondering how they got here, or stayed here. Surely when the Republic closed up the castle, some officials would have come in and helped themselves to the treasure trove, but obviously not. The candlesticks are gold too, and beautifully wrought. They must be immensely valuable. It's hard to imagine all this wealth just sitting here for decades, if not centuries.

Another oddity I just noticed is that the curtains and upholstery materials on the furniture and windows are made of very costly fabrics and must have been of tremendous value when they were originally manufactured. They are certainly old, and really belong in a museum, because they are in such perfect condition, only a little dusty.

With all the display of wealth and

luxury, however, there is one thing I notice that is missing: mirrors. There are no mirrors anywhere. I had half-expected silvered glass or polished silverplate to hang on the walls, especially in the toilet closet, but there are none to be found. I had to use my little traveling mirror to shave today. It was a bit awkward and I nicked myself slightly, but in the long run I managed.

I just heard a sound that reminded me of last night — the howling of a wolf rose from outside a moment ago. Ah, there's another, and another. I wonder if it is the same pack that surrounded our cart last night? Possibly. I regret now that I don't have a gun, with which I could at least have frightened them off.

Last night both Carolyn and Victoria remarked at my bravery in the face of a wolf pack. If only they knew. I must make a mental note to keep my journal from them, at least for a while. I don't think a man should share every secret with his wife, especially a confession of fear. Victoria believes me to be the bravest of men, and the strongest, both physically and emotionally, and I would like for her to keep on thinking so.

I have looked about for something to read. In the library off the sitting room I found many books printed both in England and in America, believe it or not. There are whole shelves of them, and bound volumes of magazines and newspapers. The table in the middle of the library is stacked high with journals and periodicals, though not of recent date, unfortunately.

The books and periodicals are varied indeed — history, geography, political science, geology, law, botany, biology — all relating to life, customs and manners in England and America. Included in the collection are books on noted personalities of the past and present, including a fairly current *Who's Who* from 1969.

Petrof has just now come in with Olga. They tell me that both Victoria and Carolyn are stirring and will be in shortly to have their breakfast. I'm rather glad because I am anxious to see more of this place.

'Good morning,' Carolyn greeted me as she came into the sitting room. 'I see you didn't oversleep like Victoria and I.'

'I must confess I just got up a little bit ago,' I told her.

'I wonder what there is about this place that seems to require sleep. It's so restful here.'

'Restful?' I raised my eyebrows. 'I thought it gave you the creeps.'

'That was last night. You know,' Carolyn said, stuffing brown bread and cheese into her mouth, 'this old place doesn't look half so bad during the day.'

'It's almost night again,' I said, glancing toward the windows.

She looked in that direction too. 'Yes, I guess it is, but it is still quite bright out.'

'It won't be for long. The night falls very rapidly here in the Carpathians, I'm given to understand. One minute it's light and the next minute it's dark as pitch. It happens almost before you know it.'

'How very odd.' Carolyn concentrated on the cold breakfast buffet.

'Everything about Castle Drakul is odd, in my opinion,' Victoria said, coming in and kissing me on the cheek. 'Good morning, darling.'

She looked lovely. The sleep had certainly agreed with her. There was color in her cheeks and her hair had never shone with such brilliance, or so I thought. I suddenly felt romantic and had to smile at myself. I felt the strangest stirrings inside me. I hadn't remembered a sensation like that since I was a lustful lad of seventeen.

I took Victoria's hand and pressed my lips into the open palm. She got my message. I could tell when our eyes met. She was blushing.

'You fall asleep too easily and get up too early,' she whispered, grinning sheepishly.

She went to the breakfast table and sat across from Carolyn. I joined them, pouring myself a cup of what the Romanians believe to be American-style coffee. At least they call it American coffee, but believe me there is no similarity.

'I thought we might start exploring the underground passages as soon as you've finished eating,' I said to Carolyn.

Victoria shivered, but Carolyn grinned

and said brightly, 'Anything you say, boss.'

'If you two are going to go roaming about this old barn, I'm going with you,' Victoria said bravely. 'I don't want to be left alone, at least not until I've gotten more accustomed to things.'

'I thought if we started with the rock samples from the cellars at the front of the castle and gradually worked our way toward the lee side of the mountains, we would be able to judge earth movement and geological composition,' I said.

Carolyn leaned towards me. 'As long as we are cooped up here, John, and as long as I am supposed to be your assistant, I suppose it might help if you explained to me just what causes earthquakes anyway. The commies might start asking me questions, so maybe you had better fill me in on a few things.'

I was sure Carolyn wouldn't understand any of it, but it made me feel good that she was at least interested enough to ask.

Victoria got up from her chair. 'If you two are going to get all technical,' she said, 'I'm going to slip into a pair of jeans so I won't ruin this dress in the cellars.'

She left the room. Carolyn sat and waited for me to explain.

'Well,' I started, speaking slowly, 'plates of rocks make up the outer layers of the earth. These rocks are continually being squeezed and stretched by forces from within the earth, forces that probably come from the enormous heat of the earth's interior. When the strain becomes greater than the plates can bear, they break or shift and cause an earthquake. It's as simple as that.'

Carolyn nodded. 'So it's because of the mountains that we've come here. The heat of the earth's interior is greater as one goes deeper, right?'

I chuckled. 'Something like that. But it isn't only heat that contributes to the earthquake. Sound waves have a lot to do with it too.'

'Sound waves?'

'Yes. Compression or longitudinal waves are really sound waves and travel at a speed of about five miles a second. The rocks vibrate in the direction traveled by the wave. This causes the rocks to change volume. Now, there are also what are known as shear or transverse waves that travel about half as fast as the compression waves. The rocks vibrate at right angles to the direction traveled by the shear waves and this causes the rocks to change shape. These compression waves and shear waves are what you may have heard referred to as seismic waves.'

'Oh, yes, I've heard of seismic waves.'

I grinned. 'Seismic waves, seismograph, seismology — the study of earthquakes.'

Carolyn sighed. 'You make it all sound so simple, but I'm sure there are a lot more things to consider than the whatchamacallit waves.'

'Indeed there are,' I said with a laugh. 'A lot more. An awful lot more, and quite a bit of it is still unknown to us. That's why I'm here in the Carpathian Mountains.'

'Well, spare me the boring details,' Carolyn said abruptly. 'I'll leave that stuff up to you. Just tell me what you want me to do, and I'll try to do it.'

'You won't find any of it very difficult,'

I said. 'If anything, I'd afraid it will all prove very tedious and boring.'

Her sudden change in attitude astonished me. One minute she was very anxious to be informed, and a few seconds later she was bored and restless and clearly disinterested. She wasn't at all like her older sister. Victoria was sensible and honest, and if she didn't want to know about something she didn't pretend interest in it.

On the other hand, if Victoria wanted to know about something, she wanted to know absolutely everything there was to know about the subject. I shrugged away the thought, however. Perhaps I was prejudiced against Carolyn simply because I was very much in love with her sister, my wife. As I watched Carolyn resume eating, one word popped into my mind: 'scatterbrain'.

'Well, here I am,' Victoria announced, coming back into the sitting room. She was dressed in an old pair of blue jeans, a plaid shirt and with a scarf tied about her hair. 'Aren't you going to change, Carolyn?' she asked.

A strange look came over Carolyn's

face. 'What for?' she asked.

'You aren't really dressed for digging around in dirty old cellars, you know,' Victoria said with a smile. 'You look more like you're off on a date.'

'Maybe I am,' Carolyn said offhandedly.

'What on earth does that mean?'

Carolyn shrugged and got up from the table. 'Let's go if we're going,' she said.

Victoria threw me a helpless glance and we followed Carolyn out of the room.

'Which door do you think leads to the cellars?' Carolyn asked, going from door to door on the first floor and trying the knobs. 'These are all locked.'

'Maybe we'll have to get the keys from Petrof,' Victoria said. She too tried a door and found it locked.

As if summoned, Petrof appeared behind me. I saw him so unexpectedly that he startled me. 'Oh, Petrof,' I said, 'it seems these doors are all locked. Do you have the keys? I'd like to gain access to the cellars.'

'There are no keys to these doors,' he said.

There was a certain glint in his eyes that made me doubt he was telling the truth, but I was not about to make an issue of it. 'Then fetch me a crowbar, or something to force a door. 'I'm sure these doors open onto the stairway that leads down to the cellars. I've been sent to investigate the underground and I can't very well do that unless I can reach it, now can I?'

I held Petrof's stare. He made no move to fetch a crowbar. 'Your ministry expects a report from me,' I said. 'I want to give them that report, but I won't be able to unless I receive the cooperation necessary.'

The expression in Petrof's eyes changed from hostility to fear. I suppose it was the word 'ministry' that did it. He went scurrying off. We kept trying door after door, but every passage was locked and inaccessible.

5

John Hamilton's Journal

Finally Petrof returned, but empty-handed. He motioned to us. 'If you must investigate the cellars,' he said, 'you will kindly follow me. There is a passage this way.'

He was looking at me as though he had just won a private victory over me. He had not produced the keys I had asked for, nor the requested crowbar. I had been prevented from seeing beyond these locked doors.

Yet he had made available to me that which I had come to the castle for — access to the underground rooms and passages. He was gloating. I understood now why some of these people are disliked by outsiders. Petrof was not a very likable individual.

The passage that Petrof showed us was cut into the side of the wall under the curve of the main staircase, the one that stretched upward from the central hallway, and the one sagging under the weight of huge cobwebs and debris.

I carried a flashlight, and when Petrof pushed open the door, I flicked on the switch and took the lead. I felt Victoria's hand tighten in mine, and I knew instinctively that her other hand was in Carolyn's.

Now I knew how Orpheus felt going into the underground in search of Eurydice. Strong as it was, my flashlight didn't seem to help much. Carolyn was the first to notice the heavy torches spaced along the walls. I began lighting them as I descended, using my cigarette lighter, but even the flaming light of the torches did not make the place less forbidding or ominous.

Halfway down the steep stone stairs, Victoria sank her nails into my hand and stifled a scream. 'A rat,' she said, half-apologizing for losing her nerve. 'It ran over my foot.'

I patted her hand and pulled her closer to me. I myself was feeling slightly unnerved by the gloomy passage. I had expected to be working under the earth, but I had anticipated tunnels or caves or caverns, and not manmade cellars, particularly cellars and passages such as the ones we found ourselves in.

Gray dust lay everywhere. Here and there along the walls were torture devices of every kind and description. Some still held the bones of victims. Victoria and Carolyn were careful to avert their eyes, but it would have been impossible to ignore them completely.

Rusted chains and manacles hung suspended from the stone walls. Iron maidens, thumbscrews and racks lined the corridor into which we had descended. The bones of humans and sub-humans — monkeys, at a guess, or apes — were scattered about, and the place reeked with the smell of decay and dankness. I did not want to be fanciful, but there was an unmistakable aura of death hanging in the cellar like a fog.

I lit yet another torch. As the flame flared, I saw that the corridor we had been walking through came to an abrupt end only a short distance ahead. A large metal-studded door stood closed before us. A tiny barred window was cut halfway up the door. The iron ring that served as a latch was rusted solid.

'The end of the line,' Carolyn said, crowding in on Victoria and me.

'Seems like it,' I said. 'But let's see what's behind this door.'

Victoria grabbed my arm. 'No, John,' she said in a tight little gasp.

I patted her hand again. 'It's okay, darling. It's just another chamber. I don't imagine it can be much grimmer than this one.'

'It is,' she said, her eyes suddenly large with fright.

'How can you know that?' I asked.

'I just do. I feel there is something horrible behind that door.'

'Nonsense,' I said. 'Come on, hold on to me.'

Victoria hesitated for a moment more, but Carolyn nudged her and she went along, huddled in our little band.

With my free hand I took hold of the rusty iron ring, and to my surprise I realized that the door was slightly ajar. I shouldered the massive panels and tried to inch the door open. It wouldn't budge. Like the iron ring, the hinges were rusted solid.

I strained against the wood, exerting more strength, and finally with a desperate shove opened the door further. The movement of the door and the screech of the hinges sent a scurry of bats flying over our heads. Victoria and Carolyn screamed in unison, and Carolyn covered her hair with her hands. The flying creatures disappeared down the corridor and up the stairs we had just descended.

'Oh, dear,' Carolyn said, struggling to get her breathing back to normal, 'those little monsters just flew up into the castle. They're probably going to nest in our bedrooms.'

'Thanks for that bright thought,' Victoria said with a note of friendly sarcasm in her voice.

I managed to inch the door open a little more, enough to squeeze around it. I shined my flashlight around the walls, searching for a torch, and found one just inside the door. I took it down and lit it. The flame sputtered and rose. The light spread slowly through the room. I moved beyond the door, and Victoria and Carolyn came in behind me, moving slowly and apprehensively.

Victoria gasped and pointed. A coffin sat in the middle of the musty old room.

6

John Hamilton's Journal

October 9th

The sight of a coffin would certainly have been bad enough, but this one was open, and the skeleton of a man lay in what must once have been his flesh. Victoria turned white. Strangely enough, Carolyn seemed fascinated. I shined my light over the naked, dry bones.

'Who do you think it was?' Carolyn asked, leaning forward and peering inside.

'Oh, Carolyn,' Victoria gasped, 'let's not look in that thing. I think I'm going to be ill.'

Carolyn ignored her. 'It's a man, there's no doubt about that, from the bone structure,' she said.

'Carolyn, please,' Victoria moaned. Then she tugged at my arm. 'John, let's get out of here. I really do feel a bit faint.'

'Victoria, for heaven's sake,' Carolyn said impatiently, 'it's just an old coffin with some bones in it.' She studied the skeleton for a moment longer. 'I'll bet he was a good-looking devil in his day.'

'Carolyn,' Victoria said, 'I must insist.'

'Try to relax, Victoria,' I said, patting her hand gently. I did not want to leave. Like Carolyn, I was fascinated, not so much by the skeleton itself, but by the length of wood that was lodged between the ribs of his rib cage. 'Can you hang on for just a moment longer, Victoria? I'd like to see why that spear or stake, or whatever it is, is resting between the ribs.'

Carolyn, to my absolute surprise, chuckled. 'It's not resting between his ribs, John,' she said lightly. 'It's a stake that was driven through the poor old dear's heart. See, it's sticking out just about where his heart would have been.' Victoria groaned at this pronouncement, and I felt her sag more heavily against me.

'Nonsense,' I said, flashing my light over the stake. 'It looks more as if it were used to prop open the lid or something.'

But the lid was not hinged, the sort that would need propping open; the lid was the sliding type and it was resting now on its side next to the box.

'John, please take me away,' Victoria pleaded, clutching tightly to my arm. 'I can't stand to look at that thing. I think it is absolutely grotesque.'

Carolyn gave her sister a displeased look. 'Don't be such a scaredy cat, Victoria. It certainly can't do you any harm.'

Carolyn's sharp admonition caused Victoria to bite down on her lip. I knew the mannerism well. It was a little thing Victoria often did. I had seen her guilty of it time and time again. It meant that she was angry, but mostly with herself. I suspected that this time her annoyance had something to do with the fact that she was showing weakness in the face of Carolyn's show of strength.

Carolyn took a step closer to the casket. 'Do you think it might be true?' she asked, half to herself and half to us.

'What?'

'That story about Drakul . . . his being

a vampire and all.'

'Oh, do talk sense, Carolyn,' I said in a stern voice. 'There are no such things as vampires, surely you know that.'

She might not even have heard me. She was staring at the skeleton so unblinkingly that, if I hadn't known better, I would have thought she was purposely hypnotizing herself — or being hypnotized. She had a strange light in her eyes and her face was completely vacant of expression. She looked odd, very odd indeed.

'They killed vampires by driving stakes through their hearts, didn't they?' Carolyn asked in a slow, even voice. She sounded as though she were talking through a heavy veil.

I felt Victoria shudder beside me, but she didn't say a word. I knew she was fighting to keep her courage.

'Nonsense,' I said.

'If you think it is such utter nonsense, John, why don't you pull out the stake and let us see what happens,' Carolyn said in that hazy, dreamlike voice.

Victoria clung to my arm. 'No, John,'

she said in an urgent whisper. 'Leave it alone. Let's go upstairs, please. This place is getting to me.'

Carolyn laughed softly. 'There isn't anything to fear down here. Not while that stake is positioned through Drakul's heart.'

'Carolyn, stop it,' I said in a stern voice. 'You are upsetting Victoria.'

'Victoria?' Carolyn still stared intently at the skeleton. Her voice had changed. It did not sound like her own at all. It was as if someone else was talking through her. 'Is it Victoria you are afraid for, John? Or are you afraid for yourself?'

'Afraid? I? Don't be absurd. What should I be afraid of? I've seen many a corpse and skeleton at the university. I grew quite used to them long ago, and believe me, I am certainly not afraid of a dried-up old skeleton like this one.'

'Well, if you are not afraid, then pull out the stake. 'Pull it out, John.'

'Why should I?'

'I want to see if way down deep inside you don't really believe in the old superstitions about vampires.'

'You surprise me, Carolyn,' I said, taking a step closer to the coffin and laying my hand on the stake. The wood felt smooth despite its crudeness, and oddly warm. It fit my hand perfectly. 'You are smart enough to know that as a scientist, mythology and superstition have no place in my life.'

'Then pull out the stake, John,' Carolyn said in a defiant tone of voice.

'No,' Victoria said, tugging my hand away from the wooden stake. She scowled at her sister. 'What's gotten into you, Carolyn? Let's get out of here right now. I have had just about enough of this silliness.'

Carolyn gave a surprisingly coarse laugh. 'So you're the one who really believes the old myth about the stake rendering the vampire dead and harmless.'

'If it pleases you to think so, that is fine with me,' Victoria said. 'However, the truth of the matter is that while I do not believe in vampires, I do believe one's last resting place should be left alone. I say leave the stake where it is and let us go upstairs.'

I am afraid now that I felt I had to side with Carolyn. Victoria, I could see, really did believe in the old vampire superstitions. That set my teeth on edge. Now I would have to prove to her that the vampire nonsense could not be true.

For all her education and her level-headedness, Victoria still had some pretty old-fashioned ideas. I would hardly believe it — Victoria was superstitious. I had never known that before, but there wasn't the least doubt about it at the moment. I could tell by looking at her that she really did believe that these were the remains of the Drakul vampire, and that the stake was keeping the vampire at bay.

I am a scientist both in mind and in body, and I simply could not permit my wife to continue to harbor such a ridiculous notion. The only way to disprove the myth was to pull out the stake and set it aside. Again, I took hold of it.

'No, John,' Victoria pleaded. 'Leave it alone, please.' Her nails were digging into my arm.

'I am merely doing this to show you how preposterous you are in believing that this bunch of old bones is the dead Count Drakul, the vampire of the Carpathian Mountains.'

The stake had begun to feel hot in my hand, and was rapidly getting hotter and hotter, until I felt that I could not hold on to it much longer. Before I was fully conscious of what I was doing, I found I had yanked the stake out with a quick jerk.

At that precise moment, however, my ears deceived me, for I thought I heard a man groan, as though with pain, or perhaps pleasure. It was an eerie sound and made my skin prickle, but I felt sure it was merely the stake scraping against bone as it came free, causing a vibration.

The moment I pulled the stake free of the skeleton, the wood turned cold, ice cold. I tossed it aside. As it hit the floor, Carolyn sagged as if someone had lifted a great weight from her shoulders.

'Carolyn,' Victoria cried anxiously.

Carolyn passed her hand over her eyes. 'Sorry, I felt faint for just a moment,' she said weakly.

'Of course you did,' Victoria said. She

gave me a hard look. 'Take us upstairs, John. We've had enough of this.' She looked with distaste at the coffin.

I shrugged and nodded toward the skeleton. 'I only wanted you to see that this hocus-pocus about vampires is just that, hocus-pocus. See, the skeleton isn't turning back into a human.'

I said that with a laugh, yet there was something about the dry collection of bones that disturbed me. They looked different somehow — younger, newer. Without knowing why, I lifted the heavy lid and managed to slide it over the coffin. Once the skeleton was out of sight, I felt a little better.

'All right,' I said, 'I think we've had enough for the time being. I'll come back down tomorrow during the daylight. Vampires sleep during the day, so the count won't be able to hurt me then.'

'John, don't talk like that,' Victoria said as we retraced our steps. 'It makes me shiver just to think about that old skeleton with the stake through its heart.'

I left the door to the coffin room open. I could see no earthly reason to close it.

One by one we extinguished the wall torches as we went back along the cold, clammy corridor. I could not help noticing that Carolyn had grown quiet.

7

John Hamilton's Journal

Steven Petrof was waiting for us. He gave us a suspicious look as we came back up the stairs, but we passed him by without a word. Olga was with him, and she pushed the door to the cellar shut in our wake and turned the key. I thought she looked frightened, but she said nothing.

That Olga was frightened, however, was confirmed a bit later. We were seated around the library, watching the Petrofs prepare the dining table. I happened to mention the skeleton and the stake to Carolyn.

'I don't understand why you were so insistent that I pull that stake out of him,' I said to her.

At this, Olga dropped a handful of the gold dinner plates. They went clattering down onto the slab floor. Her husband said something to her in a language I did not understand, and Olga scurried away.

She did not reappear at all that night.

What was stranger still was that Carolyn apparently had only the vaguest memories of that time we had spent in the cellar. She barely remembered seeing the coffin or the skeleton, and seemed to recall nothing about the wooden stake, or goading me to remove it.

Carolyn is a bit scatterbrained, true, but she has always had a keen memory. It is difficult to grasp that she would not remember something as mind-boggling as an open coffin containing the remains of a human being. I know I for one will never forget what we discovered in the cellar, and I am certain Victoria will not. Despite what I had told the two women of having seen skeletons and corpses aplenty, this particular one had made a singular impression on me. I would not exactly say that it had frightened me, but there had been something quite ominous about it, something disturbing that left me uneasy. It was all very mysterious.

At one point in the evening, Carolyn made a very morbid comment. She said that the skeleton had reminded her of

Walter. What a strange thing to say! I'm glad that Victoria was out of the room just then and did not hear the remark. I'm sure she would not have appreciated hearing Carolyn say such a thing. I know how highly Victoria regards Walter. I think she looks upon him as her brother-in-law already. She certainly would not like to hear Carolyn compare Walter to someone dead and gone.

'What was that?' Carolyn asked, suddenly sitting straight up in her chair and looking toward the windows.

'What was what?' I asked her.

'I thought I heard someone moan.' She settled back into her chair. 'The wind, I suppose. Or perhaps our friends the wolves are back.'

'Very likely,' I said. I saw that Petrof had finished setting out our meal and I went over to the table. 'Not paprika hendle again,' I said with a groan. Petrof gave me an angry look. I immediately looked sheepish. 'It's just that we have had it every single day since we came to your country.'

'It is our national dish,' he said curtly. He slammed down the platter he was holding and abruptly left the room.

Carolyn and I exchanged guilty glances. 'I'm afraid you've offended him,' she said.

'I must admit I'm a little sick and tired of paprika hendle,' I said. 'If they only knew what it does to my stomach. It keeps me up at night.'

Victoria had come into the room to hear the end of the conversation. 'You must be talking about their national dish,' she said, taking note of the dinner on the table. 'I thought so. It gives John nightmares, I'm afraid.' As we seated ourselves, Victoria leaned over and touched my hand. 'Eat lightly, John. Perhaps it won't upset your stomach if you have just a little portion.'

'Am I to starve?' I asked petulantly, helping myself to the dish.

'Which is the worse of two evils?' Carolyn said.

I merely groaned and began eating. For some reason I was famished, paprika hendle or not.

A soft, low moaning started just outside. The three of us put down our forks in unison and stared at each other. It was not wolves, not this moan. It was too human-sounding.

'I'll go see,' I said, and pushed back my chair.

'John, be careful,' Victoria called after me.

'Of what?' I asked over my shoulder. 'Whatever it is, it can't get in — not unless it has wings and can fly up the side of the castle.' I opened the casement window, wood for panes instead of glass. Bars covered the outside frame. 'And through iron bars,' I added, examining them. They looked to be quite sturdy.

Down below, the courtyard was clear and still. I saw no wolves and no humans, either — but as I gazed out into the night, I saw something black glide silently from a tower window. A huge bird, I thought, a hawk of some kind, or even an eagle. Did they have eagles in the Carpathians? I made a mental note to research that. I thought of the bats we had seen in the cellar. Indeed, I could see bats flying about in the moonlight outside, but this had been too large for a bat.

'Nothing,' I said aloud, looking toward the woods and beyond. 'It must have been only the wind.'

'There isn't any wind just at the moment,' Carolyn said.

'Whatever it was, it's gone now.' Suddenly I blinked and looked again. I saw something down at the edge of the woods. A dark figure seemed to materialize from nowhere. It was a man, a man dressed all in black. He looked up at me where I was framed in the window, and in the moonlight, his face looked as white as snow.

'A man,' I said, wondering who he was and where he had come from.

Both Carolyn and Victoria got up from the table and came to stand beside me. 'Where?' Victoria asked, peering over my shoulder.

'There, near the edge of the woods,' I said, pointing.

'I don't see anything,' she said. Carolyn said nothing.

I looked again, but he had vanished as abruptly as he had appeared. It had all happened so quickly that I wondered if I hadn't imagined it. I said as much to Victoria.

'Maybe it was Petrof,' Victoria said, leaving the window, but Carolyn remained a moment longer, staring out.

'Possibly,' I said. I rejoined Victoria at the table. Just then, we heard that low moaning sound again. It sent a shiver down my spine.

'Carolyn, do close the window,' Victoria said. 'You'll catch your death of cold.' Carolyn obeyed without a word and joined us at the table.

'Did you see anything out there?' I asked her.

'See anything?' She helped herself to more paprika hendle.

'Yes, outside.'

'Outside? No, I saw nothing.'

I had the impression that she wasn't telling the truth. I could tell by the look in her eyes that she had seen something and didn't want to admit it. But what? What could Carolyn possible wish to hide from us? Surely I was letting my imagination run away with me.

Later —

I can't help but think of Carolyn's strange behavior during the past few hours.

And who was that strange figure I saw

at the edge of the woods? I was convinced that it hadn't only been my imagination; there had been someone down there. I'm afraid that all thoughts of earthquake causation and prevention have been swept out of my head for the present. The castle is taking on a whole new atmosphere for me. I can't reconcile science and Castle Drakul. They now seem to me to be worlds apart. I scold myself for thinking such ridiculous thoughts, but they persist.

Victoria is finally sleeping soundly. She tried to sleep earlier but complained that she was either overtired or not tired enough, she couldn't decide which. We went to bed at a respectable hour, but after a time in bed we both decided we had slept too long during the day and therefore could not sleep now. Strange how our sleeping habits have changed. We seem destined to stay up at night and sleep during the day.

Dawn will be here shortly. How quiet and lovely it is here at this hour of the morning. I am reminded of the Wolf's Glen in Weber's wonderful opera, *Der Freischutz* — desolate and yet beautiful at the same time. Trees struggle up from between rocks, ghostly moonlight floods the scene. I can almost hear the voices of invisible spirits chanting to Caspar as he arranges his circle of black stones about the skull and readies himself for the appearance of the Black Huntsman, Satan himself.

I just heard the howling of wolves again. The woods must be full of them. I went to the window, staring out again. A heavy mist has come up. I almost think I can see shapes forming in it.

But, wait, it can't be true! I must be imagining it — but, no, they are there all right, down there in the trees, and coming toward the castle. Three, no, four women, dressed all in white. They are walking through the mist, almost as if they were mist themselves, and they are coming in the direction of Castle Drakul. They must be the same women Victoria saw along the road. But what in the world are they doing walking about out there in the cold? Surely they will freeze to death.

They have come into the courtyard and they are looking right up at me . . . but, wait, they're gone. They've vanished. I can't see them anywhere. Oh, this is ridiculous, they must be out there somewhere. The mist has grown thicker again. I can hardly see the stones of the courtyard now.

I have just returned from downstairs. I can't understand any of it. I was too curious to simply ignore four women in white prowling about in the courtyard, seeming to appear and disappear at will. I went down to investigate, but I had better learn to stay inside at night around here. As I opened the front door and stepped into the courtyard, a pack of wolves started to come toward me from the woods, and I quickly went back inside and shut and bolted the door.

I had seen nothing of the strange women in the courtyard, however. Like Victoria, I must have imagined them. The mist was obviously playing tricks. Those wolves were real enough, in any event. Damn but they have fierce, evil eyes. I hope they never get any closer to me than they were tonight.

Strange — now that I think of it, those

women had looked up at me with gleaming green eyes too.

John, old man, go to bed. You'll be imagining ghosts next.

8

October 9th

Dear Walter,

I suppose you'll think me strange, writing you before posting my last letter, but the truth of the matter is, you will more than likely receive several letters from me at the same time. It never occurred to me that I would have no way of posting my letters from here, but it seems we must wait for a postal wagon and I am told that only comes every week or so.

There is little to write about, except that I miss you.

John and Victoria are being very romantic. I suppose that is why I wanted to write to you again so soon.

Something very unusual happened

today. We found a coffin in one of the rooms beneath the castle. It was just sitting there in the middle of the room with a skeleton inside it. You're not going to believe this, but there was a wooden stake driven through the rib cage right where the heart would have been. Imagine! Just like in the old Bela What's-his-name movies. A real skeleton and a real stake. Do you think I might come face to face with my first live vampire? Isn't it just too exciting?

Speaking of that skeleton, I have a question to ask. Do you believe in ESP and mental telepathy and stuff like that? When I was standing over that skeleton (now don't laugh) I swear it took on flesh and blood and it was you lying there. Oh, you weren't dead or anything, you were just lying there. I was fascinated by you. Of course, if you want a girlish confession, I've been fascinated with you ever since I first met you. But I am sure you guessed that a long time ago, right?

But to get back to my old skeleton, don't you think it odd that it would change into you right before my eyes? I wonder if it means anything. Maybe it means I want you dead. Ha ha, no, that was only a joke. I'm only kidding, Walter, really I am.

Maybe after all I won't mail this letter. It's coming out sounding all wrong. It wasn't terrible to see you lying in that coffin. It gave me a kind of thrill. Am I being crazy? I mean it, Walter, I have goose bumps all over just thinking about it. It was a very wonderful sensation, like you were going to stand up at any minute and take me in your arms. Oh, I can't explain it. Believe me, though, I liked it. I liked it very much.

I'd better change the subject before you decide to send the little men in the white coats after me.

No, I don't want to see you lying in a coffin. That's not the way I get my kicks. Don't ask me to explain how I felt. I can't.

John is seeing things too. He saw some man standing beneath the window during dinner. I think I saw him too, but I'm not sure. It was all very vague and foggy when I looked out. Victoria didn't see a thing, but she wouldn't. You know how Victoria is.

Poor Victoria. She's really all nerves over this place. At least she's getting a night's sleep, which is more than I can say for John and myself. But I guess I really should try to force myself to fall asleep.

I'll write again soon.

Love as usual,
Carolyn

P.S. Stay out of drafty basements and old wooden coffins.

9

John Hamilton's Journal

October 9th, evening
I don't think I will tell Victoria and Carolyn about the Petrofs. It would only to serve to upset them unduly, since they both seem to be convinced that this Count Drakul legend has some basis in fact. Though why sane, educated people still hold fast to ancient superstition is beyond my comprehension.

Everyone knows there is no such thing as a vampire. It is a physical impossibility, and yet Victoria is convinced that the skeleton in the cellar is that of a vampire, one who existed centuries ago. She has confessed to me that she is certain I released the vampire from the prison of death when I removed the stake from its 'heart' — never mind that there was no 'heart' there, just bones and dust.

Carolyn laughs and treats the whole

thing very lightly, but I know she too believes that pile of bones was a vampire. She baffles me. She almost seems happy about the whole thing. She acts as though she is looking forward to meeting this so-called vampire.

'If one exists,' she said, but I know Carolyn is much like Victoria. Down deep she truly believes in the old superstition — or wants to.

So I will not tell them about the Petrofs. It would only add fuel to the fire of their imaginations.

Stefen and Olga came to see me earlier. They are leaving the castle. They were most apologetic about it and begged that I take my family and leave with them. In fact, I think it is some kind of ruse, a political ploy, to get me out of Castle Drakul. Perhaps they think I will back down on my earthquake investigation project, thereby giving the communists reason to complain about America's reluctance and/or refusal to help with their scientific programs.

I let the Petrofs go, and I turned a deaf ear to their jabbering about seeing a huge bat that tried to drain them of their blood. It is beyond my understanding how people can let their imaginations run so wild. But they are ignorant peasants, so I guess I shouldn't be too hard on them.

Certainly they couldn't have hoped that I would believe that ridiculous tale. First of all, if they did see a vampire bat — which I very much doubt inasmuch as vampire bats dislike cold climates — it was not huge. Vampire bats, real ones, are only three or so inches long when fully grown, and to the best of my knowledge, live primarily in South America.

Secondly, if they were attacked, the only possible danger would be that the bat infected them with rabies, of which I warned them — if bitten, they must get themselves to the nearest hospital as quickly as possible. The bat, however, could not possibly drain either of them, let alone both, of all their blood. That is a physical impossibility for so small a mammal.

And, finally, once bitten by a vampire bat, a person does not take on vampire bat tendencies, as they seem to think would happen to them. How absurd!

Nevertheless, they would not listen to logic or reason. They were convinced that they were in danger of being set upon by a gigantic vampire monster. Olga kept sobbing and blessing herself and Stefen begged me to pack up and leave before it was too late. It was quite a scene and a definite change from the dour, cold-eyed communists who greeted us when we arrived at this infernal place. Though not, I might say, a change greatly for the better.

So I let them go. What else could I do? As I said, however, I think I will keep still about their reasons for leaving and pretend to the women that they merely abandoned us. No point in alarming them unduly.

More strange happenings — about five minutes after I saw the Petrofs start off on foot, a stranger came pounding on the door. I left Victoria and Carolyn in the sitting room and went to answer the knocking. It seems we have a new host, who is to replace Skinsky. He is Count Drakul, no less. No, not that one from centuries ago, who built the castle — it could hardly be the same one, could it — but a descendant of his.

I was much flattered that he had heard of my reputation and of my coming to Romania. This being his homeland and as he was interested in my work, the government saw fit to contact him and send him here so that he could be of assistance to us. His knowledge of the castle should prove invaluable.

I told him about the Petrofs and about their unbelievable story, and I asked him if he would favor me by not mentioning their tale to my wife or Carolyn. He gave me his promise, which I thought most gentlemanly of him.

He was not too concerned about the Petrofs leaving. He said he would see that domestic help was made available. I haven't the slightest idea where he intends finding help here in this desolate region, but he assured me that he would see to it and that I must leave everything in his hands. I was happy to do so. Domestic issues could only distract me from my work.

I took him upstairs and introduced him to Victoria and Carolyn. Although he is most flattering to me and my work, I must confess I feel a strange antipathy to the man. He unnerves me by the way he looks at us, especially at Carolyn. His expression is that of a starving man at a feast table. But that makes him sound much more objectionable than he really was. I think I was still concerned over Carolyn's odd behavior, and looking for things to complain about in others.

10

Victoria Hamilton's Diary

October 10th
This place gets stranger and stranger
with every passing day. John told me that
the Petrofs are gone. Gone! Just like that.
None of us even heard them go off during
the night.

Happily, we are not completely without
help. A strange entourage attended us at
breakfast (which was served at seven
o'clock at night). A man has come to
replace Skinsky and with him is a group
of serving women. There are four women.
I could swear they are the same four
women I saw in the road the night we
arrived here, but I can't think how that
would be possible.

In any event, I asked them if I hadn't
seen them somewhere before, and all four
of them assured me that this was not
possible, as they had just come from their

village, which was some distance away, if I understood them correctly. They all four speak passable English, but with so thick an accent that sometimes I am not at all sure what they are trying to say.

The count, whose English is excellent, if accented nonetheless, tells me that they are locals who have consented to work for us during the evenings. It seems they have their own families to attend to during the day — so our day to night schedule is now completely reversed from the normal.

'But they told me they came from far away,' I said to the count, but he dismissed that with a wave of his hand.

'We are in the Carpathians. Distances are judged differently here. People from thirty, forty miles away are considered locals.'

'But how do they get back and forth if their homes are so far away?' I asked him.

'They are used to the distances. As I say, we think of them differently in this part of the world.' Which seemed to me a non-answer, but I saw no point in pursuing it with him. They were there, and we needed them now that the Petrofs had gone. I decided to let well enough alone and trust to the count.

The count . . . I must mention him. He is the strangest of the lot. His name, believe it or not, is Drakul, and he is a direct descendant of the Count Drakul who built this dilapidated castle. He — our count, that is — says he has been out of the country for several years and knew nothing about our being housed here until his government advised him of the fact.

I must say, he seems delighted to have us in his ancestral home. Personally, I think he knew we were coming here right from the beginning. I have the feeling he is just another agent for the People's Republic. They seem determined to spy on us, though I can't imagine why.

Carolyn finds the count very attractive, though I can't think why that should be either. He is far from being my type of man. He has an extremely strong face, aquiline, with a high-bridged nose that has unusually arched nostrils. His forehead is lofty and domed, with hair growing scantily at the temples but profusely elsewhere. John said it is a very intellectual skull, much like Einstein's. Never having met Mr. Einstein (although John has), I couldn't say.

The count's eyebrows are massive and thick, and almost meet over his eyes. I remember my mother once told me that when eyebrows meet like that, it means the person is very vain. That might be right insofar as Count Drakul is concerned. He seems very fond of himself. At least he gives that impression, and it is usually an accurate one, I think.

As I said earlier, Carolyn seems to be smitten with him. I can't for the life of me imagine why. I personally find him most unattractive. She says she thinks the count resembles Walter Bradshaw, but I find no physical resemblance whatsoever. The only thing they have in common is a moustache, but Walter's is very neat and tidy, whereas Count Drakul's is heavy and drooping — but it may be the sharpness of his unnaturally white teeth and the peculiar thinness of his lips that make his mustache look somehow cruel.

For the rest, his eyes are pale, his chin

broad and strong. His ears come almost to a point, and his cheeks are firm but thin. The general effect of his countenance is one of extraordinary pallor.

John has confessed to me in a whisper that for some reason the man repulses him. I can't go so far as to say that, but there is something definitely off-putting about him. Perhaps it is the fact that his name automatically conjures up unpleasant thoughts, but I don't think he can be blamed for that.

He himself has complained about how America's motion pictures exploited his family name and reduced it to salaciousness. John was quick to point out, however, that Mister Bram Stoker, who first authored the vampire stories, was British, not American. The American movie makers merely satisfied public curiosity.

Count Drakul, for all his seeming dislike of things American, has indicated an interest in closing down his old drafty castle and taking up residence in California. This sounds a bit confusing to me, as we were led to understand that the castle was the property of the government and not his to do with as he sees fit. Nevertheless, he enjoys talking at length with us about our home town. He has even hinted about his renting our California home while we stay on here. John would not hear of it, of course. I think he truly does dislike and distrust the count.

Carolyn, on the other hand, thinks we are both being unfair toward Count Drakul. Truthfully, I am of the impression that the only attraction the count holds for Carolyn is his title. She has never met any kind of royalty before, and she has always been the impressionable type. I am certain, however, that when she is back with Walter in Los Angeles she will forget all about this gloomy old castle and its strange Count Drakul. Anyway, I don't think his current government even recognizes his title, though he himself seems inordinately proud of it.

I will grant that the count has impeccable manners, however. Nothing seems to be an imposition. He is willing to do just about anything to make us comfortable and content, and I must admit he is a most interesting conversationalist. Which takes on a special importance living so far from real civilization as we are now. Of course, by civilization, I mean Los Angeles.

We had just finished eating, that first evening after he came, when the count joined us.

'You will forgive me for not having dined with you,' he apologized, 'but my stomach is most delicate and requires the blandest of foods. I eat very lightly and very rarely.'

'You need a wife to look after you,' Carolyn made bold to say.

I felt embarrassed by her remark, as did John, but the count beamed at her and took her hand.

'If I could find a wife as lovely and charming as you, my dear lady, I would be willing to settle down and bid adieu to my bachelor days forever.' He looked in John's direction. 'You American men do not realize how fortunate you are in having such beauty surrounding you. European women, certainly those here in

Romania, too often let themselves go to seed, especially after they marry.' Here he looked in my direction and added, 'But American women only become more beautiful as the years of married life pass.'

He can be a charmer, I must admit.

'We came across one of your ancestors,' Carolyn blurted out.

'Oh? And whom did you meet, may I ask, my dear?'

Carolyn shrugged. 'I don't exactly know who he was,' she said, and told him about the skeleton in the basement, and about the stake.

The count laughed. 'One of my forefathers, no doubt. My family had a strange habit of refusing to inter the dead in a crypt or mausoleum, as is usual. Instead, they often sealed up the dead in rooms below the castle. It was an old, old custom, and of course there is no shortage of rooms beneath us. Frankly, I rather approve of the custom, though it is out of step with modern notions about burial. We old Transylvanian nobles do not like to think that our bones will someday lie with the common dead.'

'*Les droit du roi*,' John muttered. 'The right of kings.'

The count gave him a cool look. 'Exactly,' he said.

'But how do you explain the stake through the man's heart?' Carolyn asked.

The count merely spread his hands in a gesture of ignorance. 'Some prank, more than likely. This old castle has been empty for many years. Travelers, tourists, come here occasionally. No doubt some roving American read the legend of the Drakul vampire and decided to add some dramatics to the tale after they found my forefather's coffin. No doubt they took pictures of it to add to the stories they would share when they returned home. Or it was meant perhaps to frighten those who came after them.'

'If that was the intent, they succeeded nicely,' I said with a shudder. 'It certainly frightened me.'

'And of course we are talking about a skeleton — a very old skeleton, it sounds like to me. You say there was a stake through his heart, but I suggest to you that there was no heart; there was a stake thrust between some ribs — who knows for what purpose?' The count smiled indulgently and turned to John. 'But enough of my ancestors. Tell me about your work, Doctor Hamilton.'

'There isn't much to tell, really,' John said. He explained briefly about the mountains and the important role they play in earthquakes. The count listened without comment, seeming completely absorbed in everything John had to say.

'Then you believe there is a possibility that this castle may someday be destroyed by an earthquake,' the count asked when John had finished his explanation. 'Buried under tons upon tons of rocks and dirt — swallowed up by the mountain?'

John nodded. 'It is more than just possible, Count Drakul. From the reports received by my government, there is a very good likelihood that this region may well be the center of a major earthquake. When that quake will occur, we cannot say, at least not at present. That is the reason I am here. The quake will come, there is little doubt of that. I mean to study the earth's crust, the various geological features of the vicinity, in order to determine the time when such an earth movement will happen.'

'You say 'will happen',' the count said. 'Then you consider it a certainty?'

Again John nodded, this time a bit more gravely than before. 'I'm afraid we cannot be one hundred percent certain. The science is not yet as exact as that. But I should say we are ninety or ninety-five percent certain. There is hardly a doubt in our minds that this castle will be destroyed by earthquake within the next quarter century, if not sooner.'

The count looked worried. 'I had no idea you scientists were so far along in your thinking.' Then he brightened and slapped his hands on his knees, standing up. 'But this old place has seen enough. Perhaps it is time for it to go back into the earth from which it was built. My family will not have the need of it.'

I frowned. His family? I did not understand and was quick to ask.

'A slip of the tongue, my dear,' he said, 'I have no family. I was referring to those dead and gone. When one becomes the last surviving member of an old and respected family, one tends to look upon the dead as still having life, and the living as being dead. I trust you understand.' He smiled at me and his sharp white teeth glittered in the light of the fire.

'Yes, of course,' I said, but in truth I did not understand. To my way of thinking, the dead are dead and the living are living, and there is no middle ground.

'But tell me all you can about America,' the count said. 'I think I should like to go there one day. I hear it is very beautiful, especially your west coast.'

'That's where we are from,' Carolyn said. 'California.'

'But I thought you said you had traveled extensively, Count,' John said with a frown. 'Surely you have journeyed to America.'

'Unfortunately, no. I have traveled extensively, yes, but perhaps not as extensively as I would wish. My sojourns have always confined themselves to the boundaries of Europe and the Far East. I have never sailed to such a distant country as your America.'

'Sailing takes too long,' Carolyn said. 'We sailed over only because of Victoria's fear of heights, but I plan on flying back. No more ships for me.'

'Flying? I'm afraid I don't understand,' the count said. He looked genuinely surprised and confused.

'The airplanes only take hours instead of days,' Carolyn said.

'Of course, of course, the airplanes,' the count said, but I could see he was still baffled. Perhaps he hadn't traveled as much as he professed to. 'I confess, when you mentioned flying, for a moment I thought you meant literally.'

A sudden thought occurred to me — perhaps he hadn't traveled at all. Perhaps our Count Drakul had been confined in some communist prison and was only recently released because he had consented to spy on us.

The more I thought about this, the more logical it seemed. He had the pale, anemic color of a prisoner. He was underweight, as if he had lacked for food. If he had been locked up for a very long time, this might explain his lack of knowledge of airplanes.

Skinsky, the Petrofs, and now Count Drakul. From the moment we had arrived in this country, the communist government has kept its eye on us. I have even begun to wonder if Drakul is a count at all, let alone a descendant of the Drakul family. Perhaps he is only a communist imposter, sent to keep an eye on us.

'It is warm in your California, yes?' he asked.

'Quite warm,' John said.

'And your house there, it is a new house?'

'Hardly,' I said with a laugh. 'John dislikes new houses. No, our home is a big old thing. It dates back to early Spanish times. We have had it remodeled, of course, some modern facilities added, but the house itself is something of an antique.'

'Good, good. I am glad your house is old and big. I myself am from a very old family, as you know, and I think if I had to live in a house that was very new and modern it would be the death of me. It seems to me that a house cannot really be made livable in one day. After all, there are but a few days in a century, true? Although I do not seek gaiety and mirth and am not eager for the bright voluptuousness of youth, I am very interested in seeing your young and warm and beautiful California. Perhaps we should exchange houses,' he said with a broad grin. 'You could stay and work here in my family's castle, for as long as you liked, and I could reside in your California home.'

He said this with a laugh but I had the impression that he was serious. I think John sensed it also because he gave the count a strange, wary look. The count recognized it too, because his expression turned grave briefly. Then he smiled again and pretended not to notice John's cold reception to his suggestion.

'Speaking of old houses,' John said, changing the subject, 'many of the rooms here in this castle are locked or inaccessible. The Petrofs told us there are no keys to the doors. Is that true?'

'Possibly. The castle has been empty for

a long time. If there are keys, they would more than likely be kept in the pantry, off of the kitchen. At least that is where the housekeepers once kept all the keys. But I would not suggest that you roam about too freely. If the rooms are locked, they are locked for a purpose. The floors are maybe sagging and in danger of collapse, or the ceilings may have fallen.'

'I was given to understand that we had full run of the castle,' John said. 'Is that not true?'

'Yes, yes of course it is true. Feel free to go anywhere you please. But my advice would be to confine your wanderings to those areas that are accessible to you.'

11

Victoria Hamilton's Diary

There was a scuffling sound in the corridor. We all turned toward the door as it creaked open. Four women, all dressed in white, stood framed in the doorway.

John rose abruptly to his feet. The glass he had been holding slipped from his shaking fingers and shattered on the floor.

The count paid no attention to the broken glass. He motioned for John to reseat himself. 'It is only the serving women,' the count said. 'I told you I would employ them for your domestic needs, did I not?'

'But . . . but . . . ' John stammered. When he regained his composure, he said to the count, 'I don't understand. You have been here with us since you arrived. How could you have arranged for servants?'

'We were sent by the Petrofs,' one of the women answered for the count.

'Yes,' another said, 'Olga told us of your

needs. We are very happy to be of assistance during the night, but during the daytime we must see to our own families.'

The count motioned toward the table, and without another word the women began to clear it.

'Are these the women you saw on the road when we were traveling here?' John asked me.

'That is possible,' the count said before I could reply. 'As I have said, they live nearby. I meant to contact these very women tomorrow, but the Petrofs have saved me the trouble.'

'But how could they? They told me . . . ' John started to say, and left his remarks unfinished.

'I think we should be thankful for small favors,' Carolyn said. 'Personally, I prefer these women to that surly Petrof and his gloomy wife.'

I had to smile, taking note of the blank expressions these women wore. They looked all of them as if they were dead on their feet. I suppose they needed the money badly, or perhaps the People's

Republic forced them to do the work whether they liked it or not.

'I can't say these ladies look much happier,' I said when they had gone out again. 'And, yes, John, I believe they are the ones I saw before.'

'And I saw them in the woods last night, after you had fallen asleep.'

The count got suddenly to his feet. 'Well, I must be about the business of getting myself settled. If you will excuse me,' he said, bowing low.

'It's odd,' John said when we were alone.

'What, darling?'

'Count Drakul. He talks of settling in, but he arrived with no luggage and he didn't come by cart or wagon or any other kind of vehicle. He just showed up, seemingly out of nowhere.'

'You can't be sure of that,' Carolyn said. 'Maybe you didn't see him drive up, but perhaps the cart dropped him and his luggage off before he knocked at the door.'

'Maybe,' John said without enthusiasm. 'The truth is, I don't much like the looks of him.'

'Neither do I,' I said, unconsciously fingering the crucifix that I pulled from its hiding place within the folds of my blouse. I had all but forgotten the crucifix that the woman at the inn had insisted I wear when she learned I was coming to Castle Drakul. Just now, touching it, I felt a kind of solace from it. The count and the four strange women have made me unaccountably nervous. Things here are not what they seem, I am sure of it.

Carolyn got to her feet, giving the two of us an exasperated look. 'Maybe you folks are getting too old to appreciate the finer things in life,' she said. 'I think the count is quite sophisticated and charming.' She hugged herself.

'Oh, dear,' John sighed. He and I exchanged glances. We both knew what the other was thinking — Carolyn was building up to one of her moods. She was being adolescent again.

12

John Hamilton's Journal

October 12th

I've started serious work on the geology report for the International Geophysical Society. I see I have let two days elapse since last writing in this journal. My reports to I.G.S. have taken precedence over this personal account.

This place is far more desolate than I had thought, and yet I have not journeyed far from the castle. The terrain is impossible. Every fragment of information is obtained only through a great deal of work and sweat. The mountains and landscape are very reluctant to part with their secrets.

We are still sleeping late into the day. No doubt this is partly to blame for the slowness with which my work progresses. I must make a concerted effort to get to bed earlier and start work in the morning when the light is at its best.

I have not gone back to the cellars. I have been spending my time out of doors. However, once the light fails, I am forced to stop. The wolves are an ever-present danger after dark. More than once as evening approached, I have seen them gliding about in the nearby forests like leaves in the wind. They have stayed their distance, but I have not lingered outside after sundown.

I wish now that we had arrived here during the daytime hours. Possibly we would not then have fallen into the habit of sleeping during the day and staying up until dawn. It is an unnatural schedule for us, and I think it is beginning to take its toll on Carolyn and Victoria. Carolyn especially looks drawn and pale these past few days. No doubt from lack of sunshine. Victoria looks tired but her color is still good, unlike Carolyn's. I really should think of sending them away. This place cannot be good for them, and the count and his strange flock of women don't help matters.

Speaking of Count Drakul, he is forever

underfoot. He follows me everywhere. Like the rest of us, he has adopted the habit of sleeping during the day and staying up until dawn. He excuses this by saying that he enjoys being waited upon and that the serving women are only available during the night.

When do they sleep? I wonder. Surely they don't leave here at dawn and go directly home to work for their families. They must sleep sometime, but when? I questioned the count about this, and he merely remarked that they manage and that I should not concern myself about the lot of the peasants. 'They are made of strong stock,' was his only explanation. He really is a snob, I fear.

At first I was flattered by his interest in my work, but now I find it is rapidly becoming tedious to have him constantly at my elbow. He watches my every move with avid interest.

I wonder where he is just at this moment. I have gotten up a little earlier than usual, but not much earlier. Since the count arrived, he has been here in the sitting room, waiting for us when we arise; but today he is absent. I confess, I am rather grateful for the fact.

But it seems I spoke too soon. He just now came into the room. I'll put this aside and go shave. I would prefer he did not see this journal.

'More reports, Doctor?' he asked as I slipped the journal back into its drawer in the desk. I turned the tiny key and dropped it into my pocket. The count chuckled at my caution. 'Have no fears of my reading your papers, my friend,' he said. 'Although I speak English, I am unfortunately unable to read it.'

I knew that he was lying. I had seen him at times reading some of the English books in the library. I chose not to answer him and went into the bedroom, where Victoria was still asleep. I did not want to disturb her, and took my shaving gear back into the sitting room. I found an alcove where the light was good, and set up my little traveling mirror and poured some hot water into my shaving mug. The count was busying himself at the table and paid me no attention.

'I'm sorry I was not here when you

woke,' he said without looking in my direction. 'I sometimes have business to attend to. If I awaken early, I often leave the castle.'

'We've gotten to be night people,' I said as I lathered up my chin. 'I wish we had arrived during the day. I'm afraid our schedule has gotten altogether off kilter.'

'I prefer your schedule as it is,' the count said. 'It corresponds more fully with my own.'

'I'm afraid we will not be able to maintain it,' I said. 'I simply must start getting up earlier. I can't carry on with my work at night. I need daylight to see what I am doing. It's impossible for me to work in the dark, not to mention that as soon as the sun goes down, the wolves come around.'

'We shall work by the light of the torches, and the torches will keep the wolves away.'

I could not get a good look at myself in the mirror where it was on the ledge, and I hung it instead from the window latch.

'How long will your work take, Doctor?' the count asked.

'Not more than a few weeks.' I looked into the mirror — and froze. The reflection in the glass showed me the entire room behind me, but I could not see the count. I saw the dining table, the chairs, the library, the fireplace — but not Count Drakul.

Impossible, I told myself, turning around and nicking myself with the razor as I did so. But, yes, there he was, standing beside the chair at the head of the table. Quickly I looked again into the mirror, and as before, he disappeared. I saw the chair at the head of the table, but no one standing beside it. Count Drakul was not to be seen in the glass. The only face there was my own.

I stood there, startled beyond comprehension. This added to the growing dread I had begun to feel in the count's company. How was it possible that I could not see him in the mirror?

The next minute, however, my eyes went to the nick I had given myself with the razor. It was now bleeding quite profusely. I put down my razor and began to search in my shaving kit for a styptic pencil.

The count looked at me then. His eyes widened at the sight of my blood, and they seemed to blaze with a satanic fury. He rushed at me and grabbed me. I drew back, too astonished to speak. I felt a spark of genuine fear. The look in his eyes was horrible. I thought he was going to strike me, but it was not this that frightened me. I felt sure I was stronger than he was. Rather, it was as if some demonic force held me in its grip.

I raised my arms, crossing them before my face. They threw the shadow of a cross on the opposite wall. The count's eyes went to this, and his fury passed as quickly as it had come. He took a step back from me.

'Take care,' he said, his eyes growing dull and pale again. 'Take care how you cut yourself, my friend. It is more dangerous than you might think in this country. You are not in your modern America where everything is sterilized and spotless. You might well infect yourself and find no cure. This is Romania. We are a very backward lot here.'

His eyes went to my shaving mirror. He reached out and took it down from the window latch. 'And this is the evil thing that has caused the damage. It is a foul plaything of man's vanity. Away with it.' So saying, he threw open the heavy casement window with one wrench of his bony hand and flung the glass out into the courtyard. I heard the glass shatter on the stones below. I was speechless. He was like a madman.

He slammed the window shut and without another word, withdrew from the room. I stared after him, astonished. The man was a lunatic, I told myself.

The lather was beginning to dry on my face. The light had faded, and I could not see now to finish shaving. Anyway, I would have to resort to using the bottom of my silver shaving mug, or possibly the back of my watchcase for future shaves. To say that I was annoyed is an understatement.

The count had finished laying out our breakfast before he had left the room. I ate alone, expecting Victoria or Carolyn to show up at any time, but neither of them made an appearance. As I ate, I thought about the count and his peculiar behavior. There was no accounting for it, except if I just supposed the man was mad. And what of that odd business with the mirror? Had I only imagined that he had no reflection in it?

Of one thing I was convinced — I must send Carolyn and Victoria back to America. They could not stay here in this castle with a mentally deranged communist one-time nobleman. Even if the count were not insane, I no longer could feel comfortable in his presence, nor feel sure of their safety.

Moreover, I have noticed that Carolyn is becoming entirely too friendly with the count. No good could come of that, I felt certain. She may think she is only harmlessly flirting with him, fascinated by his old-world aristocratic manner, but I can see the look in the count's eyes whenever Carolyn is near. He is not merely returning her flirtatious glances. I fear the count is truly interested in her. I would bet my soul on it.

'John,' Victoria said sleepily, coming

into the room, 'you're up early.'

I was sipping coffee. 'I'm going to make a determined effort to get up at dawn in the future, instead of going to bed at dawn. I simply must get more work done. I've accomplished so little since we've been here.'

'But we've only been here a few days. I think you've done quite well in getting those dispatches off in so short a time.'

'They were purely preliminary reports. I knew the post wagon would be coming through, so I wrote the I.G.S., but actually I told them nothing because I have nothing to tell.'

'And I suppose we are no help. I wish we could be, though.'

I went to her and kissed her temple. 'You're a great help to me just being here,' I told her, but I did not mean it. I felt I was deceiving her. I decided honesty would be better. 'Victoria, I've been thinking . . . '

'Yes, John?'

'What would you say if I were to send you and Carolyn back home?'

Victoria threw down the napkin she

had just picked up. 'John, no, you can't stay here all alone. Why, you just got done saying — '

'I know, I know,' I said, waving her off, but she would not be stilled.

'You just cannot stay here alone, John, you cannot.'

'I wouldn't be alone. The count is here.'

Victoria grimaced. 'A lot of consolation that is.'

'I grant you it is very little consolation, but at least he is company. He relieves the boredom, and you can't tell me this place isn't boring.'

'Well, this hasn't been the most exciting few days of my life,' she admitted with a smile, 'but at least we have each other. It's rare we have so much time together. Frankly, I am enjoying that.'

'Enjoying what?' Carolyn asked, coming into the room. I noticed that she looked even paler than she had the day before. She had lost her customary bright sparkle. I had to admit that Carolyn looked ill.

'John thinks you and I should be sent packing,' Victoria said.

'No, absolutely not,' Carolyn said.

She said it so resolutely that both Victoria and I stared at her in spite of ourselves. I saw that Victoria, too, had noticed how ill Carolyn looked.

Victoria sat at the table and helped herself to a piece of toast. 'That's what I said. I know it's dull around here, but the rest is assuredly doing us good.'

'Is it?' I asked, glancing at Carolyn. Victoria got my meaning. I began to fidget. 'I think I made a big mistake in bringing the two of you here. My work will keep me occupied too much of the time, and you will be left to fend for yourselves in this gloomy castle. In all seriousness, I think it best if you two should start packing to go home.'

'I am not leaving here,' Carolyn said sharply, 'and that is final.'

Victoria put her hand on Carolyn's. 'Perhaps John is right, dear. Maybe it is best if we go. I hate to think about leaving John, and I dread the journey back, but — '

'No!' Carolyn actually shouted. 'It's impossible.'

'Why is it impossible?' I asked her.

'I will not leave Count Drakul,' she said.

It was as I had feared. I faced her squarely. 'I thought as much,' I said impatiently. 'I had a feeling you were getting in a bit over your head, young lady. Well, I am not going to stand idly by and watch you make a fool of yourself. He'll only use you, Carolyn. He'll hurt you. I cannot permit that to happen. I am responsible for you, it's my fault that you are here.'

'Kindly mind your own business,' Carolyn spat at me.

'Carolyn!' Victoria was shocked at the outburst. She looked as if her sister had suddenly become a stranger to her.

'Leave me alone, Victoria. I am nearly of age and I am quite capable of looking out for my own affairs. I will not have you or your husband interfering with my life.'

'Carolyn, John is not trying to interfere,' Victoria said, remaining calm with a visible effort of will. 'He has your best interests at heart. After all, you hardly know this Count Drakul. He only came here a few days ago. You know nothing about him. You can't really be serious about him.'

Carolyn turned on her. 'And what if I told you that I *am* serious about him? Deadly serious? What if I told you that the count and I are . . . ' But she did not finish whatever she had been about to say.

I murmured, 'I think deadly serious is the right phrase.' If she heard me, Carolyn pretended that she had not.

'Carolyn . . . ' Victoria's hand went to the crucifix on its gold chain.

Carolyn's eyes automatically followed Victoria's fingers. Suddenly Carolyn burst into sobs. She shoved back her chair, knocking it to the floor, and dashed from the room.

Victoria jumped up, as if to go after her, but I said, 'No, leave her alone. I think she wants to be alone. And perhaps she should be.'

'Yes, perhaps you're right.' Victoria dropped into her chair again, looking utterly defeated. 'I had no idea, John. Did you?'

'I suspected something was going on,

but I had no idea it had gone so far. I could see that the count was interested in Carolyn, but I thought she was only amusing herself. Heaven knows there's little enough amusement for her here.' I went to Victoria and took her hand. 'That is why I thought it best that you and Carolyn should leave. Please try to help me convince her that she should go back to California and Walter Bradshaw.'

'I'll try when she's calmer,' she said, 'and see if I can talk her into returning to California. But we had better not mention Walter's name. Carolyn can be awfully contrary. If she gets the sense that we approve of Walter and not the count, she may side with the count just to spite us.'

'The count,' I said in an unhappy voice. 'He gives me the willies, if you want to know the truth. Do you know, I was shaving just a short while ago; and as I propped the mirror up on the window to catch the light, I looked into the glass, and I swear the count cast no reflection in it. How could that even be possible?'

Victoria gasped and stared, horror-stricken, at me. The blood drained from her face and again she clutched her crucifix. 'But, don't you know . . . according to the legends, vampires cast no reflection.'

I could have kicked myself for telling her that. Now I really had managed to frighten her. But the damage was done, there was nothing I could do to change that.

The door opened, and we both turned in that direction. The four serving women stood just inside the room. 'Have you finished your meal?' one of them asked.

Victoria seemed unable to speak. 'Yes, you may clear things away,' I said.

The count entered on the heels of the ladies. Victoria gave an involuntary gasp when she saw him.

'Good evening, Victoria,' the count greeted her in his usual suave manner. She still did not speak. 'Is there something wrong, my dear?'

Before Victoria could answer, I said, 'I'm afraid Victoria and Carolyn had a slight quarrel.'

'A quarrel?' I thought the count was smiling, but I could not be certain. Could he know what the quarrel had been about? I wondered.

'Nothing serious,' I said. 'Just a slight misunderstanding.' I helped Victoria up from her chair. 'Darling, why don't you go to your room for a moment? I would like to speak to Count Drakul privately.'

Victoria offered no resistance. She might have been walking in her sleep, but she did as I suggested and returned to her bedroom.

'And what do you wish to speak to me about, Doctor?' the count asked when she had gone.

I glanced toward the women still clearing the table. The count snapped his fingers, scowled at them, and motioned toward the door. The ladies filed out hurriedly, almost scurrying.

'Carolyn,' I said bluntly when we were alone, 'I'm afraid I will have to ask your assistance with a rather delicate situation.'

'Whatever I can do to help, I will be most happy to do,' the count said.

'I don't know how to broach the subject, but I suppose the best way is the direct way. It seems that my dear innocent little sister-in-law is infatuated with you.'

The count laughed as I knew he would. 'Charming, charming,' he said.

'Not so charming,' I replied. 'Carolyn is a very impressionable young lady. She is engaged to a young man in Los Angeles, California. You would be doing my wife and me a great favor it you would not encourage Carolyn. As I said, she is impressionable and very young, as you can see. You are a man of experience, no doubt. I'm sure you know how to discourage such unsuitable situations as this.'

The count regarded me for a long moment. 'But why should I want to discourage it?' he asked finally. 'I find Carolyn quite delightful. I am most flattered that she has fallen in love with me.'

'I did not say she had fallen in love with you,' I replied in my sternest voice. Even to my own ears I sounded like a disgruntled father. 'I said she was infatuated with you. There's a difference.'

The count shrugged indifferently. 'Often the only difference is the amount of time involved. Infatuations usually develop into love, given enough time.'

'And that is exactly what I want to avoid,' I told him.

'Why? Do you disapprove of me, Doctor?'

'As a suitor for Carolyn, yes. You know very well that anything serious developing between you and my sister-in-law would be most, shall we say, inconvenient. We are from different cultures, different societies. You are European nobility. Carolyn is middle-class American. You are a communist. We are democratic. It would not be practical for things to get out of hand.'

The expression on his face was so smug I was tempted to put my fist into it.

'I'm sorry, my friend. I admit that I am a few years Carolyn's senior. Other than that, I see nothing unusual about a love affair developing between us. Even the difference in our ages is not particularly significant. Here in Europe, it is not at all unusual for young women to marry men many years older than themselves. It gives the young lady security, stability.'

I was dumbfounded. 'You can't mean that you intend encouraging Carolyn?'

'Perhaps. In any event, I see no reason

to discourage her.'

'My dear count, think of Carolyn. You aren't really serious about her. I thought at first you might be, but now I can see that you are merely toying with her affections.'

'You may be right,' he admitted bluntly. 'But in all frankness, Doctor Hamilton, I cannot see what business it is of yours.'

I exploded. 'Carolyn is part of my family. So long as we are here, she is my responsibility. I have every right to interfere in this matter. Why, the girl isn't twenty-one years of age yet.'

'I was of the impression that Americans achieve their majority at age eighteen,' he said.

'Not in all matters. Since her parents are gone, Victoria is her guardian. She cannot marry without Victoria's consent until she is twenty-one.'

'But that is in California. According to our laws, she can marry whomever she wishes. And whenever.'

I could feel my face getting hotter and hotter. 'I tell you, I won't permit this to continue.'

'Since there is nothing you can do about it, I suggest that you tend to your own business and not mine or Carolyn's. It will do you no good to interfere.'

'We shall see about that.'

'Yes, the count said, pausing dramatically. 'We shall see about that.' He bowed again and left the room.

13

Letter from Miss Carolyn Stuart to Mr. Walter Bradshaw, Los Angeles, California, U.S.A.

October 12th
  Walter,
Get out of my life. I never want to see you again. Never! Never! Never! I hate you!

Oh, no, Walter. Help me, in the name of heaven, help me!
                                                    C.

Victoria Hamilton's Diary

October 12th
  He casts no reflection! Oh my God, what have we gotten ourselves mixed up in? I am frightened, really frightened. I had a feeling that something dreadful might happen ever since John found that

hideous coffin in the cellar — ever since he pulled the stake out from the skeleton's heart.

Oh, I know he will say that I am talking insanity; that there are no such things as vampires. But he is wrong. With all John's scientific knowledge, how can he explain the fact that the count casts no reflection in a mirror?

I was reluctant to face my fears before this, but now I must face them and I must warn everyone. They will have to believe me. I will *make* them believe me. How could I have been so blind for so long? The warnings of the villagers, the legends, our mysterious sleeping schedule: awake at night, asleep during the day — it all fits together with the tales I've read and heard about vampires. I know it is all true now, fantastic as it may seem.

And Carolyn? We must get her away from here. She is in the clutches of that fiend, I know she is. I know my sister very well, and I have been aware for the past few days that she has not been herself. Since Drakul showed up here, she has been flirtatious and gay, and flippant to the point of insincerity. And yet for all her unnatural gaiety and supposed happiness, she has daily become more drawn and pale.

I thought at first her pallor was due to the fact that she is not getting any sunshine, what with sleeping until dark and staying up until the dawn; but now I know better. It isn't the lack of sun, it is the fact that Drakul and Carolyn — oh, I can't bear to write it. I don't even want to think about such a horrible thing, even though in my heart I know it is true.

I must make John believe me. I must warn him. I know he is as concerned as I am for Carolyn, but I am afraid he will not face the ugly truth. He believes Carolyn to be simply infatuated with Count Drakul. He does not realize that Carolyn cannot help herself. We must get her away from here. We must!

I can hear John and the count talking in the next room. Talking? No, their voices are raised; at least John's is. So they aren't talking, they are arguing.

We are so far away from home. I wish we had never come. No, I don't mean that. John had to come. It is best that we came with him. Left to himself here in this terrible castle, Lord only knows what might have happened to him. He would have found that casket by himself. The Petrofs would have deserted him, and he would have been left entirely at the count's mercy. At least we are a party of three. There is safety in numbers, they say.

John just stormed into the bedroom, slamming the door after himself.

'John,' I said anxiously, getting up from the writing desk, 'what is it? What were you and the count fighting about?'

John clenched and unclenched his fists as he paced back and forth, running his hands through his hair from time to time. 'What else? Your little sister, of course,' he said. 'Drakul is an egomaniac. That man is actually delighted that a young innocent girl like Carolyn is attracted to him. He intends to encourage her.' His face was scarlet with rage. 'He even hinted at marriage. Can you imagine the nerve of him?'

The expression of worry and anger on John's face made me momentarily forget about vampires — but only momentarily.

I thought of Carolyn. She was innocent in what was happening. It was obvious to me that the count had her under his hellish spell. John must not accuse her unjustly or think ill of her.

'We must get Carolyn away from here,' I said anxiously.

I couldn't share my fears with John yet. He would only scoff at them. His trained scientific mind would refuse to accept the beliefs that my mind harbored. I would have to work this out alone, at least for the time being. Our first move, however, must be to somehow force Carolyn to leave — even if we had to spirit her away. Yes, even if it had to be done against her will, for her will was no longer her own.

Idly my fingers toyed with the tiny gold crucifix resting on my bosom. Of course, I thought, as John continued his pacing back and force — the crucifix had saved me from the count's clutches. He would not have dared to approach me so long as I wore it.

Surely it would protect Carolyn as well. I must give it to her to wear. I have John to protect me. I don't really need the crucifix. I would make Carolyn wear it instead.

I racked my brain trying to remember everything that I had ever heard about vampires. What protected you against them? I bit down on my lower lip and tried to think. Religious articles warded them off; that I knew. All evil was afraid of the symbols of good. I would get my Bible from my suitcase and keep it with me at all times.

I was sure, though, that there were other kinds of deterrents. Yes, wolf's bane, or a wreath of garlic worn round the neck. But where on earth would I find garlic and wolf's bane here in the Carpathian Mountains? Certainly not in this castle. I would have to rely on the Bible and the crucifix.

In all my ruminations, I had not been listening to what John was saying. Now he stopped directly in front of me and said, 'We'll have to put a stop to it somehow, Victoria. We are strangers here, in a country whose relations with our own are not of the warmest. We can't afford to get mixed up with the count's government and his politics. Carolyn must simply be made to see reason. She's just being headstrong and stubborn. She doesn't really care a fig about the count. Well, I will not tolerate it, Victoria, I simply will not tolerate it.' He slammed a fist down hard on the writing desk.

'John, John,' I said, surprised at my own sudden calm. I felt that I had already solved the problem. 'We will take Carolyn home as soon as possible. It's the only thing to do. You know very well that she is not herself.' I hesitated, screwing up my courage for the argument John would no doubt launch the moment he heard me out.

'There's more to this situation than meets the eye,' I said, and again hesitated, wary. 'Those stories about vampires — they are true, John. I know they are.'

He stared at me briefly, unbelieving. 'Oh, Victoria, be sensible. Please don't start inventing a lot of nonsense simply to justify your sister's irresponsible behavior.'

'I'm not inventing anything. As a scientist, you must agree that there are many, many things in the world that are unexplainable.'

'Of course there are, but certainly not vampires and werewolves and the so-called undead.'

'Why not? You said yourself that the count did not cast a reflection in your shaving mirror. Explain to me why he did not, without facing the possibility that Count Drakul is what everyone says he is — a vampire.' My voice had begun to quiver.

'A vampire?' John snorted his disbelief. 'Really, Victoria, I'm beginning to think you are as addled as Carolyn.'

'I'm not addled, John, and I am not being ridiculous. I'm merely facing the truth.'

'Vampirism? Victoria, I am surprised at you.'

'I know, I know,' I said, holding my hands up. 'I too thought vampires were a lot of nonsense, until I began putting things together.'

'What things?'

'The way Carolyn is behaving toward the count. The way she looks — anemic. The coffin with the stake in it. The looks of horror on people's faces whenever this

145

castle was mentioned. He shuns the day-light. And the final touch was your discovery that the count casts no reflection in a mirror. Surely you must have noticed there are no mirrors here in the castle; none. What other explanation can there be for all those things, except that he is a vampire, he and those strange women who appear only at night? Those women don't live with their families. They *are* his family. There are no other houses around here, we saw that on the drive in; no families nearby for them to go home to. Don't you recall what Skinsky told us — there are no other houses here where we might have stayed? That was why they housed us here, in this castle.' My voice was rising. I knew that I sounded very close to panic.

'Victoria,' John said sharply, taking me by the shoulders, 'stop it. You're talking nonsense.'

'John, you must listen to me.'

'Not another word. I agree with you on one point, however — we must get Carolyn out of here. I'm sending you both back as soon as possible. Immediately, if it can be arranged. I will speak to the count. He must have some way of contacting his government.' John started from the room.

'No,' I cried, rushing at him and throwing myself into his arms. 'Oh, John, no, don't tell the count. We must leave, all of us, right away. But don't tell Drakul of our plans. He'll do something horrible, I know he will. We can sneak away without his knowing that we've gone.'

'We?'

'Yes, all of us. We must get away from here before it is too late.'

'Oh Victoria, do be sensible, please. You know very well that I cannot leave here with my work undone. In any case, the local government did not want us to come here in the first place. I seriously doubt that they would permit us to just pick up and leave.'

'You must. You can't stay here now, John. Count Drakul will — '

'Victoria, I refuse to listen to any more of this silliness. Don't ask me to explain why I did not see the count's reflection in my shaving mirror. Maybe I did not have it tilted at the right angle, or maybe it was just a trick of the light, or even a flaw in the glass. Whatever it was, I am sure there is a perfectly good explanation for it. It was not because Drakul is a vampire, I can assure you.'

'John, listen to me,' I implored him.

'No, not another word. I am going to arrange for you and Carolyn to leave as soon as possible.'

I couldn't let him do this — I had to stop him. He could not stay here alone with the count. 'I'm not going,' I said in a determined voice. John whirled around to face me. 'If you're staying, then I am staying with you.'

'You are leaving, Victoria, you and Carolyn both.'

'No. I can be as stubborn as you.' I was staring hard at him, my chin jutting out in defiance. This was for his own good. 'I will not leave you here alone.'

'Victoria, I do not want to have a scene. You will do as I say.' He turned again and stormed out.

I stood dazed and frightened. He was going to tell the count that we were leaving — but he must not do that. If he knew of our plans, the count would never let us leave. I rushed after him, but he was gone, gone in search of Count Drakul.

I thought of Carolyn. Perhaps if I got her away first, then I could return to protect John from his own stubbornness. Yes, I must think of Carolyn first. For the moment, she was the one in the greatest danger.

I hurried through the sitting room toward Carolyn's bedroom, my hand already undoing the clasp of the crucifix as I went. But her bedroom was empty. I stood in the doorway, remembering her burst of tears and her flight to this room. I had half-expected to find her sprawled on the bed, eyes red, mouth pouting — but she wasn't here. I went through to the little toilet closet. The door stood ajar. The closet was empty.

I heard a sound behind me and turned to find John there. 'She isn't here?' he asked.

'No.' I made a gesture that took in the empty bedroom.

'I can't find the count either. They are most likely together. Come on, we must find them.'

'John, wait,' I said, but he did not wait. I had to hurry to keep up with him. I called after him as he started down the stairway that led to the first level: 'Where are you going?'

He didn't slow. 'Drakul must occupy the Petroffs' old apartment off the kitchen,' he said. 'Where else could they be?'

'We mustn't tell the count of our plans,' I pleaded. 'Let's just find Carolyn and confer among ourselves. Don't say anything to the count. Please, for my sake.'

John didn't answer. He hurried down the long dusty stairway and turned toward the kitchen. Halfway across the foyer we heard a soft, girlish laugh. It was Carolyn's. It came from behind closed double doors that had been locked when we had tried them before.

'Come on,' John said in an angry voice. He did not bother to knock or announce himself, but took hold of the doors and flung them open.

Carolyn and Count Drakul were sprawled on a divan in what could only be described as a compromising position. My hand flew to my mouth and I gasped — but it was not the sight of Carolyn's impropriety that made me gasp. The count's mouth was at her throat. He appeared to be biting her.

'Carolyn,' John barked, 'go to your room.'

'Oh, bother,' she said, sitting up and adjusting the neckline of her blouse. 'Why do you always have to spoil my fun? You sound like the father in some old-time melodrama. Can't you just leave me alone and mind your own business?'

I frowned. This was not the Carolyn I knew and loved. This was some stranger before us. She got to her feet and swayed unsteadily. If I didn't know better, I would have said that she was inebriated. She took a step forward and almost lost her balance. The count steadied her and eased her toward us. He wore a sickening grin on his face.

I knew that John's temper was ready to erupt. Unconsciously, I raised the tiny gold cross I had taken from around my neck. I was standing just behind John, so he did not see what I was doing.

As I raised the crucifix, Count Drakul's eyes widened. He suddenly cowered in fear and, covering his face with his hands, he slunk out of the room. I watched him go with a sinking feeling in my stomach.

I was right. There was no longer any doubt about it. Drakul is a vampire.

14

John Hamilton's Journal

October 12th

My assignment is finished almost before I have started it. I have decided that we will leave Castle Drakul and return home, regardless of the consequences. It is clear that if we stay, the consequences will be far graver.

Carolyn is behaving most shamefully. Plus, she does not appear to be in good health. She is pale and drawn. My biggest concern, however, is her infatuation with the count, which seems to be completely out of hand. Tonight Victoria and I found them in a most indelicate situation in a downstairs drawing room.

I have ordered Carolyn and Victoria to pack immediately. We will leave in the morning, as soon as I can make arrangements for our departure with Count Drakul. I am sure his government will be most unhappy, but that cannot be helped. My family's welfare must come first.

Victoria, too, is becoming a bit strange. She keeps talking about vampires, and she is convinced that Drakul is that pile of bones we discovered in the coffin, although they had not a shred of flesh on them. I've tried to reason with her, in vain. Knowing Victoria, the more I try to talk sense into her, the more stubborn she will become. It is probably best if I do not contradict her ideas. She will put them aside in good time, when we are far away from here.

It is certainly not because I believe Count Drakul to be a vampire that I have decided to leave. On the contrary, I consider him all too human, and not a very good human at that. His behavior with Carolyn this evening was the final blow. She is young and innocent, and I will not have her corrupted by some communist one-time nobleman.

As for the count, he seems to have disappeared. He is usually underfoot until dawn; but after that scene in the drawing room he rushed away, and I have not yet been able to speak to him about our leaving.

It was out of character for the count to slink away like he did. We had a heated discussion earlier about Carolyn and he certainly stood his ground then. Why then did he run away when we caught him red-handed? I expected him to stand up to me as he had earlier. He's a very strange man, and one I would prefer to see no more after tomorrow. The man is unscrupulous and without a shred of moral fiber.

I intend to wait here for Drakul if it takes all night. I know he will show up sooner or later. He always has, and I see no reason for him to change his schedule now. I have a strong feeling that he will try to see Carolyn again or that she will try to see him. I intend to prevent such a rendezvous. There will be no further opportunities for them to continue their little intrigue behind our backs.

Carolyn is probably right in saying that I am acting like the irate father in some old silent movie, but I can't help that. It is for her own good. Can't she see that? I know Victoria does.

Dear Victoria. What would I do without her? I rant and rave at her, and she tolerates my ill temper and moody disposition. If she wants to go on believing that Count Drakul is a vampire, all well and good; I will let her continue believing it. In that way I will have no opposition from her about getting out of this blasted place and away from that unsavory Drakul.

The four serving women just came in. Now there's a quartet for you. I asked them if they had seen the count. They did not even answer. They just looked at me with those pale, lifeless eyes and shook their heads. I thought one of them smiled at me just now, but perhaps I imagined it. I can't trust my imagination these days.

'John,' Victoria called softly from the doorway to Carolyn's bedroom, 'can you come here for a moment, please?' She cast a cautious eye on the serving women.

I got up from the desk and went to her. She did not say a word until we were in Carolyn's bedroom and the door closed. She looked worried.

'What is it?' I asked.

She glanced toward Carolyn, who was standing at the window, gazing out into the blackness of the night. 'She's acting strangely,' Victoria said. 'I'm afraid for her.'

'What do you mean, strangely?'

'Talk to her. You'll see what I mean. Talk to her about Count Drakul.'

I did not want to talk to Carolyn about Count Drakul, but the frightened look in Victoria's eyes melted my resistance. I went over to Carolyn and put my around about her. She did not move a muscle.

'How are you feeling, Carolyn?' I asked her. 'I hope you aren't too upset with me.'

She turned slowly, looking as innocent as a fresh flower. 'Upset with you? But why should I be, John?'

'That business with Drakul,' I started, feeling most uncomfortable.

'What business is that?' She looked at me with wide eyes.

'Downstairs, in the drawing room.'

'Drawing room?' She shook her head. 'I haven't been in any drawing room. I'm afraid I don't know what you're talking about.' She gave me a weak smile and turned back to the window to resume her study of the night beyond.

I glanced at Victoria, who motioned me to her.

'She doesn't seem to remember any of it,' Victoria whispered. 'It's as if she has blocked it from her mind. She's in some sort of daze.'

'A temporary emotional block,' I said with a frown. 'It will pass.'

'Will it?' Victoria asked, sounding unconvinced.

I could not trust myself to answer.

October 13th

The strange business with Carolyn gave me a sleepless night, or should I say a sleepless day. Here it is, evening again, and I have been up for almost an hour. Drakul has still not made an appearance.

We must be up and away from this place tonight. He must make the arrangements, even though Victoria begs me not alert him to our intention of leaving. I must tell him, and not simply because it is the honest thing to do. I can't slink away, as he did last night. I'm not that sort. In any case, it would not be possible for us to go without enlisting his assistance in making the arrangements. We can hardly start out on foot in these mountains.

In all truth, I dislike the thought of leaving. I have never quit a project before, and I do not like quitting this one. Yet regardless of the scientific importance of my work, I feel that my family's well-being must be my first concern.

I should never have allowed myself the luxury of bringing them with me, but that is water under the dam, and it does no good to fret over past mistakes. I had no idea that the location would turn out to be so very remote, so austere. I had expected isolation, of course, but not desolation. This is no place for Victoria and Carolyn. I have only myself to blame for what has happened.

Ah, finally, Count Drakul has come in. Or did he materialize? I heard no door open. (I'm letting Victoria's nonsense get to me.)

'Good evening, Doctor Hamilton,' the count greeted me. 'I trust you are well this evening.'

'Very well, thank you, Count. I have a favor to ask of you.'

He was grinning in that devilish way he had. 'Anything, dear doctor. You have but to name it.'

'We are leaving, tonight if possible, and I hoped that you — '

The count looked at me with disdain. 'Impossible,' he said in an imperious voice. 'You cannot leave.'

'We can and we intend to do so,' I answered him firmly.

'You do not know what you are saying, Doctor. You cannot just walk out of here. This is not America and you are not a tourist.'

I settled back in my chair, ready for the arguments I was sure he would offer. 'I realize that there may be ramifications,' I said, 'but it cannot be helped. In view of what has happened, I have no other recourse but to take my family away from here.' I narrowed my eyes. 'You know, of course, to what I refer.'

The count gave me one of his smug smiles and fanned out his hands as if brushing away my remark. 'An innocent tête-à-tête,' he said. 'You are making a mountain out of a molehill.'

'I do not agree with you, Count Drakul, and I am very concerned for my sister-in-law's well-being. I look upon the incident with much disfavor. Moreover, I do not think Carolyn is well. I think I must take her away from here.'

The count chuckled. I despised him for his insolence.

'You think unkindly of me, I know, Doctor — but regardless of what you think of me personally, it must have no bearing whatsoever on the work you have come here to do. I am sure our governments will not approve of your leaving before the project is complete.'

I squared my shoulders and prepared to stand my ground. 'I am equally sure that our governments will understand when I place the facts before them.'

The count continued to smile in a condescending manner. 'Your government, perhaps. But mine?' He fanned out his hands again. His eyes glinted like steel darts. 'I cannot be sure they are going to look upon your departure with favor.'

He was trying to browbeat me, but I refused to let him. 'You can't threaten me, Count. I have no doubt that you will do everything you can to besmirch my reputation, but I do not really care. As long as my family is left unblemished, that is all I care about. You are a corrupt and a no-good scoundrel, in my opinion, and I do not intend to remain in this house another night. We are leaving as soon as it can be arranged. I don't give a hang about your political threats.'

'What political threats?' Victoria asked, coming into the room. She was dressed for traveling, which pleased me.

'You look lovely, my dear Mrs. Hamilton,' the count said, bowing to her.

She arched her eyebrows and stiffened her back. I noticed that she carried her Bible in her hand, which was not typical of her. She was religious, yes, but not to that point. I'd never seen her carry her Bible around before, except for the day we were married. When the count spoke to her, she positioned the Bible upright. I thought the count flinched slightly and took a step backward.

'I am quite well, thank you, Count,' she said in an icy voice. 'I trust you had a good night's sleep.' Her voice dripped sarcasm. She clutched the Bible tightly. It was as if the book itself was giving her strength.

The count looked uncomfortable. 'You are dressed for travel,' he said.

'Yes,' Victoria said. 'We plan to leave at once.'

The count made a slight bow. 'I must apologize, my dear,' he said, 'but I cannot permit you to leave.'

Virginia's eyes grew wide and cold. 'And why not?' she asked, hugging the Bible to her bosom.

'It has nothing to do with me personally,' the count said. 'As I was telling your husband, my government will not look kindly on your departing before the work on the earthquake project is completed.'

I took one of Victoria's hands in mind. 'And I was just telling the count that his government can go hang,' I said, pleased with myself.

The count looked at me maliciously. 'It is not as simple as you seem to think. Here in Romania, we have what might be called a controlled society. A sudden departure, in view of the importance of your work, would cause considerable dismay on the part of those members of the government who originally sanctioned your trip. There is little doubt in my mind that you would be detained until a full investigation could be made.'

Victoria and I looked at each other. Detention here meant only one thing — imprisonment. Neither of us spoke.

'Insofar as your report to the I.G.S.,' the count continued, 'there is little likelihood that it would ever reach its destination.' He had us and he knew it. He could arrange our arrest without batting an eye, and things would then be far worse for Victoria and Carolyn than they were now.

I felt defeated, and I could see that Victoria too was frightened by the possibility of our becoming political prisoners in

Romania. We could easily disappear and never be heard from again. We wouldn't be the first. Yet I had to stand up to Drakul, or try to.

'You wouldn't dare,' I told him heatedly.

'Ah, but indeed I would dare.' He chuckled again. 'I would be only too happy to do a service for my government.'

'He's bluffing, isn't he, John?' Victoria asked me.

I wished I could give her the answer she wanted to hear, but I could not. 'I'm afraid he isn't,' he said. 'He wouldn't be the first to arrange such imprisonment. It's 1946 all over again.'

Victoria looked blankly at me.

'In 1946,' I explained, 'the Communist Party took over Romania's government, and all non-communists — or for that matter, anyone who opposed them — were imprisoned or killed. They made it all very simple: death in one form or another, or communism. No, my dear, I don't think the count here is bluffing. They are a hellish lot.'

'But we're not in Russia,' Victoria said.

'This is Romania. It's only a small satellite country.'

'It makes no difference, dear. Russia controls everything here: the people, the politics, everything. Under its new constitution, Romania was made entirely dependent on Russia. Then Romania joined the Warsaw Pact, a Russian dominated military alliance. Oh, the poorer Romanians tried to assert their independence from Russia, but people like the count here made that impossible.'

'You give me too much credit, Doctor,' the count said, still smiling. 'I am not involved in local politics. I only use them to gain an end whenever necessary.'

'You monster,' Victoria cried. 'You cannot force us to stay in this horrible place.'

I patted her hand. 'I'm afraid he can,' I said, my voice heavy with defeat. 'I'm afraid he can.'

Victoria suddenly lost her composure. She threw herself into my arms. 'Oh, John, what are we going to do?' she sobbed.

'Come, come, my dear,' Drakul said.

'There is no reason to alarm yourselves. I do not particularly want to resort to involving my government.'

I gave him a frosty look. 'Not much,' I said.

'No, that is true, my good doctor.' His expression was guileless, but I could not bring myself to put any trust in this devil of a man. 'The present-day Romania means little to me. I am from the old country and have little to do with the modern system. I will not resort to turning you over to the government unless you force me to, in which case I will have no other recourse. I mean you no harm. On the contrary, I can be of great benefit to you if you will permit me.'

'Don't listen to him, John, don't listen,' Victoria said.

He ignored her remarks. 'I am a Szekely,' he said instead, 'as my father before me and their fathers before them. In these veins flows the blood of many brave races who fought as the lion fights, for lordship. Centuries ago, here in the cauldron of European nationalities, the Ugric tribe carried down from Iceland the conquering spirit Thor himself gave them. The House of Drakul was foremost in inspiring other races to join in our fight to overcome the barbarians who overran the great river into the land of the Turks.

'We were beaten back time and time again but in the end we were victorious, and after the endless wars, we of the Drakul blood emerged as leaders. Ah, my good people, the Szekelys — and the Drakuls who were their heart's blood, their brains and their swords — can boast of victories greater than those of the Hapsburgs and the Romanovs, and even of the communists and your United States of America.

'Alas, the warlike times are finished for us. The glories of our great family are nothing more than another story to tell. But I can make your blood as mine. You can become lions of battle, or mental giants. You have but to say the word.'

Victoria and I stared at him. What he was saying seemed to have neither rhyme nor reason. Why was he raving about his bloodline, his ancestors? Whatever he was hinting at, we were not interested. I, at least, wanted only to be out of there, away from him and his lost ancestors, and the lot of them could hang so far as I cared.

'Finish your project, Doctor Hamilton,' the count said, again smiling as if he were savoring some devilish joke. 'Finish it quickly, and then perhaps I will have had a chance to change your mind about leaving. If not, I promise I will arrange for your departure without further ado.'

Victoria and I looked at one another. We both knew we were at his mercy. There was nothing we could do but agree to his terms.

'We must stay, John,' Victoria said. 'I don't wish to, but we have no alternative.'

'I'm afraid you are right,' I said. To Drakul I said, 'I will do as you say.'

'That is a wise decision,' he said, looking pleased with himself.

'But, there is no reason for my wife or Carolyn to remain here. You are only concerned with my project. If I stay, then you must arrange to have them sent home immediately.'

'As you wish,' the count said, bowing.

'John, no,' Victoria said. 'If you are

staying, then I will stay too. I will not be sent away. Send Carolyn, but not me.'

'Very well, Victoria, tell Carolyn to get ready.'

As if she had heard her name, Carolyn came into the room just then. She looked paler and more wasted than ever. If she had not been walking, I would have guessed her to be at death's door.

'Get ready for what?' she asked.

'To leave,' Victoria told her. 'You are going home. John and I will stay and finish his project.' Carolyn opened her mouth to say something, but Victoria cut her off. 'I won't have any arguments, Carolyn. There has been enough foolishness already, and you have been the cause of it, whether you wish to admit it or not. You're going back and that's all there is to it.'

Carolyn looked at Count Drakul. I had the impression that some silent message was communicated. When Carolyn looked back at Victoria, her eyes were more lifeless than ever. 'All right,' she said, 'when do I leave?'

Her voice sounded strange. She was

taking this far too calmly, I thought. Victoria and I looked suspiciously at one another. I felt sure something was brewing, but I couldn't think what it might be.

'I will arrange for a wagon to be brought up,' the count said, going toward the door. 'It should be here in a few hours. In the meantime, dear Carolyn, I would suggest you pack your belongings.'

'Yes, of course,' she said. 'If that is what you wish.'

'That is what I wish.' He went out.

Carolyn disappeared into her bedroom, closing the door.

'Now what?' Victoria asked when we were alone.

'You're going with Carolyn,' I told her.

'I am not, John. I refuse to leave you here.'

'Victoria, be sensible. Nothing is going to happen to me.' I took her in my arms. The truth was, I did not want her to leave me, but I knew it was for the best.

'Please let me stay. I can help with your work, and we'll finish it that much sooner.'

I kissed her hair. 'I want you to stay, darling, you know that I do. But I don't trust the count. And the communists are a tricky bunch.'

'But don't you see? With me here, the chances are they won't try anything. They would be foolish to detain an important scientist and his wife after the project is concluded. It would create an international scandal. And with Carolyn safely back home, she could tell the world the truth. You must let me stay with you. It's the only way.'

In the face of her determination, I relented. 'All right, darling, if it means so much to you.'

'It does,' she said happily. We kissed to seal our bargain.

'At least Carolyn is leaving,' I said with a sigh. 'And Drakul isn't putting up much of a fight about it. Which is strange, though.' I paused and rubbed my chin. 'I wonder why he is so calm now about her leaving, after our row last night. What has changed his mind?'

'I'm sure he's up to something,' she said. 'I can't believe he will let Carolyn out of his clutches so easily. But at least I still have my Bible.'

'What has your Bible to do with anything?'

'The Bible and my gold cross are our only protection against him.'

'Ah, now I understand. It's that vampire business again.'

'Don't scoff, John. I'm serious. We must keep the Bible with us at all times. I gave Carolyn the crucifix for her protection.'

A loud crash from the direction of Carolyn's room interrupted our conversation. We rushed to her door, but it was locked. Victoria pounded on the door, crying, 'Carolyn, Carolyn!'

The lock clicked and we heard the sliding back of the bolt. The knob turned and the door opened slowly, to reveal Count Drakul.

'I'm afraid Carolyn fainted,' he said. 'I've taken the liberty of placing her on the bed. But do not be alarmed. It is nothing serious. She seems to have come down with a slight fever. This happens often to tourists who are not used to our environment. It will pass shortly.'

'But she was to leave,' Victoria said.

'And so she shall, in another day or two. For now, however, she must rest.'

Victoria stopped down and picked up something from the floor — a broken gold chain. The tiny cross it had held before was nowhere to be seen.

Despite Drakul's words and my own protestations, I was suddenly afraid, afraid for all of us.

15

John Hamilton's Journal

October 14th
  Last night I forced myself to retire early so that I might also rise early and get started in earnest on my project. For the first time since coming here, I got up before nine o'clock in the morning. The day is magnificent, too, so clear and bright and fresh. The morning sun washes away the musty darkness of the castle.
  This is in fact a beautiful place when one sees it in the daylight. Pine trees grow everywhere and in every shade of green, and the sight of the blue-purple mountains standing row upon row is breathtaking. I am almost tempted to wake Victoria so that she may share the beauty with me.
  There is no one about. It is obvious that no one expected me to start my day so early. Unless I find myself something to eat, I'm afraid I will have to go without breakfast.

I looked in on Carolyn. The poor girl looks absolutely terrible. Her pallor is death-like; there is no other word to describe it. She is still running a fever. I did not want to disturb her. No doubt sleep is the best remedy. Victoria will go to her when she wakes. I left the door to our bedroom and the door to Carolyn's open, just in case Carolyn wakes and calls out.

My footsteps echoed through the empty halls as I made my way down the wide stone staircase. Everything was quiet. No one was moving about. I found some cheese and bread in the kitchen and ate some, wrapping more in a napkin and stuffing that into my kit. I checked my equipment before leaving the castle. All was in order and I set out, convinced that I could finish the work quickly.

Beyond the cold, barren courtyard, mighty forests sloped up to the lofty heights of the Carpathians themselves. The mountains towered all around, the bright morning sun falling full on them and bringing out all the magnificent colors — deep blue and purple, green and brown, granite-colored rock mingled in an endless perspective of pointed crags and jagged cliffs. Snow-covered peaks stood high above. Through an occasional rift in the mountains I could see the gleam of stately waterfalls. Birds chirped merrily. I felt alive for the first time in days. For the moment I forgot about the castle behind me, and Count Drakul.

I crossed the tree line and the sun suddenly seemed to sink lower behind me. Shadows rose up, crept closer, stretched out before me. I could almost feel the chill of those snowy peaks. Gone was the warmth of the sun and the gentle breezes. Even the birds seemed to have ceased their singing. I was in the forest now, walking toward the base of the nearest mountain.

The wind grew stronger and colder as I made my way deeper into the tangle of trees and brush. My equipment felt heavier. It weighed me down. I shifted some paraphernalia from one shoulder to the other, and made a mental note to wear heavier clothes and gloves tomorrow. It was cold in this gloomy forest.

Something made me turn and look back toward Castle Drakul. It was fortunate for me that I did so, because the castle had vanished among the trees. I could not see its turrets or its spire.

I carefully retraced my steps until I once again caught a glimpse of the castle. Then, so that I would not lose my way, I began to break branches and uproot shrubs, to leave a trail for myself. It would not do to get lost in this infernal place, especially since I knew that night fell quickly and it was not safe to be abroad after dark.

I hadn't gone more than a few hundred yards, once again headed toward the base of the mountain, when I saw them and froze in my tracks. I felt my stomach churn and had to avert my eyes from the grisly scene.

Stefen and Olga Petrof — dead, of course; I did not have to examine them to determine that. They were grotesque, lying on their backs, their faces turned toward the sky they would never again see. Their expressions were the most horrible I had ever seen: blind terror imprinted on their faces, their eyes bulging, their mouths agape in silence screams. Their clothes, even their limbs, were in shreds, their throats torn open, as though by some monstrous animal; and the ground around them was stained with dried blood. I felt certain they had been set upon by the wolves.

When my stomach turned over, I looked away and retched up the small bit I'd eaten for breakfast. My instinct was to run away from this gory sight. But I still had work to do, and that was important if we were ever going to be allowed to leave here. I turned my eyes away and hurried past the bodies.

When I was well beyond them, I knelt and said a silent prayer for the souls of the dead couple. I prayed as well for my safety, and for Victoria's and Carolyn's. Then I rose and went doggedly about my work.

As an aid to help take my mind off the Petrofs, I began to talk aloud to myself. I went over the procedure I would follow once I reached the foot of the mountain and had set up my equipment. I checked and counted off the sticks of dynamite I had brought with me.

My first step was to make a study of

the earth's crust. I would choose the locations for the dynamite and would set off the explosives above, on and below the surface. The blasts would produce sound waves that would bounce back from the rock layers at various depths before the surface. The seismograph I had with me would measure the travel time of those waves and tell me what lay beneath.

By the time I reached the first spot I had selected, the Petrofs were forgotten for the time being. I had brought the most sensitive of my seismographs, the Benioff. Tomorrow, with Victoria's help, I would bring the other two instruments.

No, I corrected myself, remembering — I could not bring Victoria here until the bodies of the dead couple had been taken away, out of sight. Victoria must not see that horrible scene.

I finished setting up the seismograph and measured out the distances for the charges and decided upon the force of the blasts. My work went well, and by one o'clock I was satisfied enough to take a recess and eat the food I had packed in my kit. I had no sooner laid out the food, however, when thoughts of the Petroffs intruded in my mind and my appetite vanished. I pushed the food away and went back to my work.

I set off the blasts and measured and recorded their effects. My findings were exciting, and again I forgot everything except the work at hand.

A cold burst of wind reminded me of the time. I looked up through the trees and saw that the sun was getting ready to quit for the day. Hurriedly I covered the equipment with canvas. I built a hasty shelter for the tools I would leave behind — I thought it unlikely that anyone would wander by, and they would be of no interest to the wolves. I wished I knew another way back to the castle so that I would not have to see the Petrofs again, but I was too afraid of losing my way to stray from the trail I had marked earlier.

My fears proved to be unfounded. When I got to where the Petrofs had lain, I stopped and stared. The bodies were gone. There was no sign of them anywhere; and, stranger still, there was no sign of them having been dragged away.

I scratched at my chin, wondering if I had mistaken the spot. But no, this was where I had seen them. I could still see scraps of clothing, bloodstains, tufts of hair. There was no question that this was where they had been. But they had mysteriously disappeared.

I did not want to think of an explanation, because the only explanation was too horrible to contemplate. The wolves, of course . . . but no, I would not think of that. I quickly got my bearings and rushed back to the castle.

Victoria was seated before the fire when I came into our sitting room. We talked briefly about my work, and I asked, 'What of Drakul? Has he shown up yet this evening?'

'No, not yet,' she said. She glanced toward the window where the sun could be seen just resting on the horizon. 'It's not quite sundown. He'll be here shortly, I'm sure.'

'Have you spoken to Carolyn?'

'Only for a moment. She rallied a while ago and stirred, but I couldn't get her to eat anything. Oh, John, I'm so worried about her. She looks dreadful.'

I thought about the grisly discovery I had made in the forest, but I couldn't tell Victoria about the Petrofs. 'We'll get her out of here as soon as we can,' I assured her. 'The work went well today; and tomorrow, if you will help, I think we can make even better progress.'

Drakul suddenly loomed beside us. I hadn't heard him come in. 'So the work went well,' he said, smiling to display his sharp white teeth. 'Splendid, splendid.'

Despite his words, I could tell just from looking at him that he was not at all pleased. 'Victoria,' I said, 'would you mind terribly if I spoke to the count in private? There is something I must discuss with him.'

She gave me a strange look. 'What on earth could you possibly have to say to the count that I shouldn't hear?'

'Please, Victoria. Why don't you go and sit with Carolyn? This will only take a few minutes.' The count regarded me suspiciously.

'If you insist,' Victoria answered reluctantly. She offered me her hand to help her out of the deep chair. I felt her slip something into my hand. When I saw that Drakul was looking after her, I glanced down. There, resting in my palm, was the tiny gold crucifix that Victoria had given Carolyn. Obviously she had found it somewhere in Carolyn's room. I closed my hand over it as the count turned his attention back to me.

'And what do you wish to discuss with me now, Doctor?'

'I went into the woods this morning and began my work, as you know.'

'Yes, but that does not exactly please me. I would prefer that you wait until I am available in the evenings, and we can accomplish the work together.'

'I don't think you'll want to work in those woods at night after you've hear what I have to say.'

'And what might that be?'

'Just before you came here, we had a pair of servants, Stefen and Olga Petrof.'

'Yes, yes, I know that. They left.'

'I found them today.'

The count smiled. 'Found them? Were they lost?'

I despised him for his levity. 'They are dead, Count Drakul. Dead. They had been set upon by some wild, vicious animals. They were torn to shreds.'

The count merely clicked his tongue in his cheek. 'Ah, that is too bad; but it only serves as a reminder of just how dangerous those woods can be. I would suggest that you wait until I can go with you before you venture again into that forest. First the Petrofs. It could be you next, Doctor Hamilton. I would be more careful if I were you.'

'Oddly, their bodies have disappeared. They were there went I went out, and not when I returned.'

'That's hardly mysterious. The wolves came back to finished their dinner.'

My stomach gave a warning turn. I sank into a chair. He had put it so indelicately. I loathed him all the more for his flippancy, and his lack of concern or respect for the two people who had died.

'Don't you intend to do anything about the Petrofs?' I asked him.

'Do? But what would you have me do?'

'Surely it should be reported — to someone.'

'Oh, I see what you mean. But what is the good of that? You say there are no longer corpses. The People's Republic would expect us to produce corpses. If none are available, I see no reason for bothering about the matter at all.'

I was shocked out of my chair. 'How can you be so heartless, so cold-blooded? Damn it, man, two people have been killed by wolves. Don't you feel you should notify the authorities so that the relatives of the deceased might at least be told?'

'Ah, you Americans are such slaves to detail and to humanitarianism.' He dismissed my complaint with a wave of his hand. 'I hope this has served as a warning. The forest here is extremely dangerous, Doctor Hamilton. I would alert the fair Carolyn and your beautiful wife to this fact, in case . . . ' He did not finish the sentence.

It was clear he did not intend to do anything about the Petrofs. I myself would make an official report at the first opportunity. For the time being, I had the count to deal with. 'If the woods are so dangerous in daylight hours, aren't they doubly so at night?'

'Not if you are with me and not if we carry torches. The wolves, like all animals, are afraid of fire. They will not attack us.'

'Nevertheless, I am afraid I cannot do as you ask,' I told him. 'This stage of my work must be done during the day, when the temperature is at its highest. Later we will record the reaction of the shock waves in night-time temperatures, but that will be the final phase of the project. I cannot wait for you to join me, Count. I intend to work tomorrow as I did today. And if it will ease your concern for my safety,' I added with dripping sarcasm, 'I will light torches and surround myself with them.'

He only shrugged. 'As you wish. But kindly remember that you were warned.' It was clear he was not at all pleased with my decision.

The serving women appeared and began to lay out the evening meal. I called to Victoria and picked up a wedge of cheese from one of the trays, purposefully pushing the Petrofs from my mind.

'Carolyn's still sleeping,' Victoria said, coming into the room. 'I hope you two have finished your chat.' She reached for my hand and I slipped the crucifix into hers.

'Yes, dear,' I said. 'Come, let's eat, and then I want to retire early. I have a busy day tomorrow. You're coming with me, aren't you?'

She nodded. I saw that Drakul was standing to one side, studying us intently. He was plotting something, I was sure.

16

Victoria Hamilton's Diary

October 14th

John is already sleeping, and I will force myself to do the same in a few minutes. Just now I am sitting with Carolyn, who is resting more easily. She awoke a few minutes ago and seems to be stronger. At least she showed an appetite, which is a good sign. I told her about John's getting started on his work, and she seemed genuinely pleased.

Carolyn is under the impression that the strange fever that beset her is the cause for her unusual behavior. I let her believe that. I know different. My suspicions of Count Drakul were confirmed when I saw the tiny marks on Carolyn's throat. I shudder to think of them. He has been feeding on her. I must be constantly on my guard until we are all out of the dreadful place.

Luckily I found the crucifix. The count must have thrown it into the corner of the room, or somehow influenced Carolyn to do so. And I keep my Bible with me at all times, knowing Drakul cannot harm me so long as I carry it. That and the little cross must be our protection.

Carolyn is sleeping soundly. I'll leave her and join John. I have tacked the cross above her bed. So long as it remains there, she will be safe from Count Drakul.

I think John is beginning to believe me. He took the crucifix without hesitation and kept it in his hand all the while he and the count were alone. Perhaps he no longer thinks my fears are so foolish.

What did he have to say in private to the count? Something happened today when he was in the forest, something John does not want to tell me about. Perhaps it has something to do with those four women. They seem to live there, in the forest. Did he come across them? I'll ask him tomorrow. I'll make him tell me.

How I wish we were away from here. Carolyn is stronger, but I am still very much afraid for her. It is obvious that she is under Drakul's control. The longer we stay here, the greater the danger for her.

I hear Drakul and the women moving about in the other room. I must go to John. We are safer together.

John Hamilton's Journal

October 15th

Well, now we know what the count was plotting last night.

Victoria and I both got up early. She made breakfast and packed our lunch, and we got ready to leave — but we didn't go far. We never left the castle, in fact.

The front door had been bolted from outside, and the key was gone from the lock. We looked about for some other way out, but the only other exit was the kitchen door, and that too was locked. The castle sits on the corner of a great rock, so that on three sides it is impregnable. To the west is a great valley, and beyond the valley, rising far away, are great jagged mountains, peak upon peak.

Most of the windows look to the south. A stone falling from any of them would drop thousands of feet before hitting anything. A sea of green treetops stretches as far as the eye can see, with an occasional deep rift where chasms cut the green. Here and there, silver threads of far-away rivers wind through narrow gorges.

The windows in our sitting room overlook the courtyard, but it is still a considerable distance to the ground. I thought about climbing out the window and jumping, but I was afraid of breaking an ankle or a leg, and thus making myself helpless and leaving Victoria and Carolyn unprotected.

Doors, doors and more doors, and all of them locked. The castle has become a veritable prison, and we its prisoners. I confess I am just as unnerved as Victoria, though I am doing my best to hide it. We have agreed that in the future, whatever we plan, we will not discuss it with Count Drakul. He won't hear a single word from either of us so far as what we are planning to do. That is of no help in our current dilemma, however.

As I sit looking out toward the south, I am reminded of the beauty of yesterday; of being outdoors in the sunlight, breathing clean, clear air, and not the musty, dank atmosphere inside this decaying old castle.

'What are we going to do?' Victoria asked.

'We'll find a way to get out,' I assured her. 'The count must have taken all the keys when he left, but there have to be ways out of the castle that he hasn't thought of. Why don't you go and sit with Carolyn, and I will look downstairs. Maybe there's a window in the cellars, or a tunnel through the walls.'

'He can't hurt us, you know, during the day. He sleeps in his coffin during the daylight hours.'

'Now, no more of that,' I said.

'But you are beginning to believe, aren't you?'

'I believe one thing,' I told her. 'That there is a mystery here, something going on around us that is not right. I just don't know what it is.'

I kissed her and left her there and went to my search of the cellars. At least the door that had given us access to the cellars before was still unlocked. I went down the long, dark flight of worn stone steps, lighting the torches as I went.

The door at the end of the corridor was still ajar. I went into that room and lit the torch just inside the door. The casket was in the same place. I did not notice immediately that the lid was no longer on it, as I had left it. The coffin was not my reason for being here. I was looking for windows or other doors that would lead us outside.

Unfortunately there weren't any windows or other doors in the room. I would have to search elsewhere.

It was as I turned, torch in hand, that my eyes fell again on the casket. I saw now that the lid was not in place. The light of the torch showed the interior of the coffin. I stared.

Count Drakul lay inside the coffin, where the skeleton had been when we had first seen it. He was neither dead nor asleep. His eyes were open and stony cold, but they did not have the glassy look of the dead. His lips were red as rosebuds. He showed no signs of movement, and when I screwed up my courage and checked for a pulse there was none. Nor was there any other sign of life, neither breath nor heartbeat. I bent over him, looking for some indication that he was living. There was none.

I stood, shocked with fear and wonder. Suddenly a rumbling sound came from the coffin. The body twitched and moved slightly. A trickle of blood seeped from between his lips and trickled from the corners of his mouth, running down over the chin and the neck. He looked completely gorged with blood. It made my stomach turn just to see the awful creature lying there like a filthy leech, exhausted and sated.

I shivered. Every fiber of my being was revolted. For the first time, I put credence in Victoria's insistence that Drakul was a vampire. I did not want to believe it. I *couldn't* believe it — it was too fantastical — but there was the evidence, right before my eyes. He lay filled with blood, sleeping through the daylight hours, waiting for night.

Things suddenly became clear in my mind. This was why he was never available during the daytime. He only moved about at night. He never ate food, as mortals do. Carolyn's malady was no fever. He had been draining her not only of her blood but of her strength and her reason. It was he who had made us prisoners, and he wanted to drain Victoria and me as he had drained Carolyn.

Or did he? What was he waiting for? Why had he given us the latitude we had enjoyed so far? Why had he kept us alive if he was only interested in the blood flowing through our veins? He must need us for something other than our blood — but what?

Drakul's face wore a mocking smile. It drove me mad. I didn't know what I was doing, but I did know that the count had to be destroyed.

Yet I couldn't bring myself to kill. I couldn't take a life, regardless of what Drakul was, even if it was a matter of my own self-preservation.

The wolves began to howl in the distance. My blood turned to ice. I could think of only one thing to do — to lock the count inside this room until I could get help. But would that do any good? Would locked doors hold Drakul? Even if I nailed down the lid of the coffin, would that be enough to prevent his leaving it?

No, I would have to rid the world of this creature before he rid the world of us. I looked around the room. There in the corner lay the stake I had yanked from his heart. I must put it back where I had found it. I had brought him back to life when I removed the stake. If I thrust it into his heart again, he would return to his deathlike state of limbo.

I picked up the stake and went back to the coffin. I put the tip of it against his chest and started to lean on it. As I did so, the head turned and his eyes flew open, eyes filled with hate, staring directly at me. The sight paralyzed me for a moment. His lips moved. The mouth opened to speak. A gurgle came from between the lips and blood bubbled out of his mouth. I was shaking from head to toe. I forced my eyes shut and braced myself against the stake.

'No, John,' a voice said from behind me.

I straightened, the stake dangling from my hands.

'Carolyn, how on earth did you get down here?' I asked. 'You should be in bed.'

'I'm feeling much better,' she said, her voice faint and vague. 'You mustn't do that, John. It will kill me too, you know.' She said this in a tone of indifference, staring at the seemingly lifeless body of Drakul in his coffin. I looked at him too, and back at Carolyn, torn by indecision.

'He must be destroyed,' I said.

'And you will then destroy me also.'

'What can I do? I must release you from his power.'

'You must not. I am his mistress.'

'Then you are the mistress of evil.'

She sighed. 'Yes, it is true. But there is nothing that I can do now to change anything.'

We heard steps in the corridor outside, and seconds later Victoria called, 'John,

John, are you down here? Carolyn's gone.'

I did not want Victoria to see the count. It was too horrible. I threw the stake aside and extinguished the torch just as Victoria pushed through the door.

'Oh, here you are,' she said when she saw Carolyn. 'You gave me a fright when I saw your bed was empty. I didn't expect to find you down here. I came for John.'

'He needed me,' Carolyn said in her ghostly voice.

Her eyes rolled up in her head then and her knees started to buckle. Just as she would have fallen to the ground, I caught her and scooped her up in my arms. Victoria gasped.

'She's only fainted,' I said. 'Come, let's get her back to bed. She shouldn't be down here in the cold and damp.'

I stood so that I was sure I was blocking Victoria's view of the coffin, but at the moment her thoughts were only of Carolyn. I breathed a sigh of relief as we made our way back up the stairs. I would have to come back another time and settle up with Count Drakul — but what of Carolyn? Would killing him mean killing her as well, as she had said? My heart sank at that prospect.

17

John Hamilton's Journal

October 15th

That sight in the basement, I can't get it out of my mind. What sort of creature is this Count Drakul? My mind refuses to accept that he is a vampire, yet what other explanation could there be? What other sort of creature would sleep all day in a coffin?

More pressing still, to my mind, was the other question — what does he want with us? His intentions toward Carolyn are no longer in question, but what of Victoria and me? He has hinted at more than just satisfying himself with our blood, though I have no doubt he will want that as well.

It is insane. This cannot be happening to us.

Victoria came in just now. I cannot let her see this journal, not until we are away from this nightmarish place.

'Carolyn wants to talk to you, John,' Victoria said. 'She's awake and asking for you.'

I gave her a suspicious look. 'Did she say anything to you about why she was downstairs or how she got there?'

'Not a word. She just woke up and started mumbling about wanting to see you; that it was important.'

I sighed with relief. Victoria had to be kept from knowing about Drakul. She would only panic.

Carolyn was lying propped up on pillows when I came into her room. Surprisingly enough, she was smiling and looked very bright and wide awake.

'I must say, you're looking much better,' I greeted her.

'And feeling it.' She glanced at Victoria, standing in the doorway. 'Dear Victoria,' she said, 'I'm positively famished. Do you think you could find something downstairs for me to eat?'

'Of course. I'll fix you a banquet fit for a queen.'

When she had gone, Carolyn reached

out for my hand. I sat down on the edge of the bed. 'I haven't thanked you for carrying me back to bed, have I?' she asked.

'That's not necessary. We can't have you wandering around in these drafty old hallways.' I wanted to asked if she remembered anything about being in the cellar — how she got there and why — but I did not get the chance.

'Then why don't you keep me warm?' she said, raising herself toward me. She winked and gave me a coy smile.

I backed away from her. Was I imagining it, or was Carolyn flirting with me? I couldn't believe that she would do so. She put her hand on my knee and began to draw tiny circles along my leg with her fingers. Her other arm went around my neck and pulled my face close to hers. Her fingers moved up my leg.

'Carolyn,' I said, shocked, 'behave yourself.'

She giggled like a child. 'You must have known how I've felt about you all these years,' she whispered. 'Ever since I was a little girl, I wanted you to hold me like this, to feel your body hard against mine.'

'Carolyn.' I struggled to free myself from her embrace. Her hands and arms were everywhere.

'Don't fight me, John. I know you want me. Take me. Love me. Kiss me. Please, make love to me, please, please, please.'

My mind was in a whirl. I was shocked and disgusted. This was not the Carolyn I knew and cared for. This was not Victoria's sister. This was yet another monster, a monster created by Count Drakul.

I drew away from her. She clung to me, trying desperately to kiss my mouth. Her hair fell back and I saw the marks on her throat. I held her wrists tightly in my hands and stared at the tiny pricks on her neck. Bite marks.

When I looked into her eyes, she was leering at me, her expression all too much like the count's. She was no longer the sweet young girl whose sister I had married; not the pleasant, charming young lady who had traveled here with us.

She was a fiend. When she smiled, she showed the same sharp white teeth as the count. The same evil expression showed in her eyes. She moved her body most voluptuously; but the more she tried to seduce me, the more disgusted and angry I became with her. 'You sent Victoria away on purpose,' I said.

She merely laughed in my face. 'Of course I did. Would you have preferred for me to seduce you with Victoria present? She doesn't frighten me, you know. Nobody does.'

'Carolyn, you don't know what you are saying.' She only smiled and tried once again to kiss my mouth. 'You must try to help yourself. Stay away from Drakul. Stay under the protection of the crucifix.' I looked up at the gold cross tacked over her bed.

She glanced up at it and recoiled. Averting her eyes, she reached up and snatched the crucifix down and threw it across the room. 'Take it away. Get it out of here,' she yelled. 'I never want to see it again.'

Victoria appeared in the doorway bearing a tray. 'What is it?' she asked. 'What's happened?' Carolyn flung herself down on the bed and gave herself up to loud sobs.

'I've got to put a stop to this,' I said, standing. I thought of the casket in the cellar, and glanced toward the windows. It was still full daylight. There would be no threat from Drakul for hours yet. I had to get to the cellar and do what was necessary to render the monster harmless.

I left the two women together and rushed down the stairs. The cellar door was closed, and when I tugged at it, it didn't budge. I rattled the latch. It was locked. Someone had locked the only door that led down to that room with its evil coffin.

But who could have locked it? There was no one else in the castle but Victoria and Carolyn and me, and Carolyn had been unconscious when we'd come up earlier. Surely Victoria would not have locked it. Was it those strange women? Or had the count, even in his deathlike sleep, done it with sheer mental force? There was little question that he had strange powers, powers of which my science knew nothing. I returned to our apartment, desolated.

Carolyn was still collapsed in Victoria's arms when I came back upstairs. 'Did you lock the door to the cellar?' I asked Victoria.

'No, of course not. Why should I lock that door?'

'I didn't ask you why, only if you locked it,' I said, speaking too sharply.

'No, I did not,' she said, just as sharply.

'It must have been those women.' I dropped into a chair. 'I'm sorry, I'm letting all this get to me.'

'It's getting to all of us,' Victoria said. 'Especially Carolyn.' She brushed stray hairs back from Carolyn's forehead.

Suddenly Carolyn threw back her head and started to laugh. We both stared at her.

'Oh, you two should see yourselves,' she mocked us. 'Why so glum? Think — we can stay here forever and never have to worry about anything again. The count will see that we are well taken care of.'

'The count,' I groaned. 'That monster is the one who should be taken care of.'

Victoria looked at me strangely. 'John,

there's something you're not telling me. You've discovered something and are keeping it from me. What is it? I have a right to know.'

'Don't. It's nothing.'

Carolyn laughed. 'Nothing, is it? I tell you Victoria, it's everything.'

Victoria looked confused. 'I don't understand.'

'You will. When we have settled down here with the count . . . '

Victoria's eyes grew larger. 'Settle down here? We are going to do no such thing.'

'But you have no choice,' Carolyn said, grinning.

I went to Victoria and put my hand on her shoulder. 'Don't listen to her. She's only trying to frighten you.'

'Tell her, John,' Carolyn said. 'She has a right to know, if she doesn't already.'

'Tell me what?' Victoria demanded.

'I am the count's mistress. And I am going to marry him. And you can't stop me. It's too late. No one can stop us.'

I suddenly realized, looking at Carolyn, hearing her obscene laughter, that she was entirely right, it was indeed too late.

She was lost to us. She was sick, but there was no cure for her disease. We were too late to save her; the count had already taken her from us.

Victoria's hand lashed out and she slapped her sister violently. Carolyn grabbed her hand and all but twisted it off. Frightened, Victoria pulled her hand away.

Carolyn tilted her head and showed us the bite marks on her throat. 'You see, I belong to him now. I will stay here forever.'

Victoria looked up to the headboard. 'The crucifix!' she cried. 'It's gone!'

'Carolyn threw it aside,' I said. I went to the corner of the room where she had thrown it and brought it back. At the sight of it, Carolyn cringed away from me. Yes, I told myself again, she was lost to us.

'It's true, isn't it, John, what I said?' Victoria asked me. 'About the count.'

I couldn't answer her. With a bowed head, I turned and went out of the room. Carolyn's mocking laughter followed me.

18

Victoria Hamilton's diary

October 15th

Night will soon be upon us. Drakul will return. Even the thought of him makes my blood run cold. John says he will insist that the count give him the keys, but I don't believe that will happen. Drakul intends to keep us here forever.

What we are to do about Carolyn, I have no idea. Carolyn has said she wants John kept away from her. She claims he tried to seduce her. Ridiculous, of course. Even if John had decided to be unfaithful, which I do not for a moment believe, it would not be with my sister. Discretion is John's middle name.

Night is here. This nocturnal existence is beginning to tell on us all.

John Hamilton's Journal

October 16th

Victoria has had a bad fright, but of course she is imagining things. What she is not imagining, however, is that we have somehow become prisoners here in Drakul's castle — a situation that I will not tolerate.

I told the count as much when he came to see us that evening. 'I will not accept being a prisoner here,' I informed him firmly. 'I insist that the doors be unlocked.'

He gave me one of those smarmy smiles I have come to hate so much. 'And so they shall be,' he replied. 'As soon as you do one small favor for me — well, in fact, two small favors.'

'What favors are those?'

He held some papers in his hand and offered them to me. 'I'll need you to sign these documents. Of course, you will fill in the proper addresses where needed.'

The first of the documents was headed:

TO THE ATTORNEYS OF JOHN HAMILTON, LOS ANGELES, CALIFORNIA, U.S.A.

Gentlemen, Please be informed and advised that I, John Hamilton, hereby appoint and designate the bearer of this letter, COUNT F. S. DRAKUL, my true and legal attorney. Count Drakul is hereby granted permission to act as my agent in all affairs on my behalf. It is my wish that Count Drakul be given my power of attorney. The count, together with whomsoever he may wish to mention, is to be given access to my house and property, located at _____, Los Angeles, California, U.S.A. He may maintain occupancy of said premises for as long as he wishes without making payment in any amount for the occupancy of said premises. All expenses incurred in the upkeep of the property will be assumed by me, and Count Drakul is be given power of attorney for my checking accounts as well as the power to act in my behalf in all other matters, financial of otherwise. On this day I hereby affix my hand and seal.

'You're mad,' I told him. 'I will never sign this.'

'I think you will. And the second letter as well. Perhaps you should read it now.'

I did so. This one was addressed to the International Geophysical Society, Romanian Branch, Bucharest, and read:

Gentlemen, My project in the Carpathian Mountains is nearing completion. I am writing to request that you grant permission to have removed from your fine country certain crates and boxes of earth samples which I would like shipped to my home address in America. These containers — which I estimate to be in number about five or six — will hold nothing but rock and earth samples that I will be able to examine more thoroughly at my laboratory there than with the necessarily limited equipment I brought here with me. I trust you will forward your permission for shipment of these parcels at your earliest convenience so that I may return to my country and continue toward completion of this vital work.

Sincerely, John Hamilton.

'Never,' I cried, flinging the papers to the floor.

'I think that you will sign them,' he said, once again smiling in that odious way at me. 'You say you want to leave here. Once you have signed those documents, you will find a horse and carriage waiting outside the unlocked front door first thing tomorrow morning.'

'That's monstrous,' I cried. 'It's blackmail.'

'Call it what you will. I see it as a simple exchange of courtesies. You sign, you go. What could be fairer than that?'

Victoria had retrieved the papers from where they had fallen on the floor and read them. She looked, horrified, at me. 'John, you couldn't possibly consider signing these,' she said.

'It appears we have no choice. Unless we do, we shall remain the count's prisoners here, perhaps forever. Give me those.'

I snatched the documents from her hands and, taking a pen from my pocket, I scrawled my signature on them, filling in the necessary blanks, and thrust them at the count. 'Here, and damn you.'

He took them and with a sigh and said, 'I fear you may be too late for that, my friend. But you will find me a man of honor. Tomorrow morning at sunrise, a horse and carriage will be waiting for you outside the front door. For now, I bid you farewell.' He made a curt little bow and strode from our apartment.

'John, how could you?' Victoria demanded when we were alone. 'You know what it means. He'll be living in our country, working his evil on unsuspecting victims . . .'

I dismissed her objections with a wave of my hand. 'Those documents mean nothing. Once we are back in Los Angeles, I can easily undo all that. What matters now is our getting away from here, and unless he breaks his word, we will be able to do so. And before we go, I intend to see that he will never again work his evil on anyone.'

'But what can you do? We have no weapons.'

I smiled at my wife. 'Ah, but we do,' I said. 'I am going to create an earthquake.'

19

John Hamilton's Journal

'And how will you do that?' she asked.

'The same way I did earlier in the forest. There are underground springs and streams below this castle. If I plant the right charges deep enough, I should be able to rock this castle — not to destroy it altogether, but to unhinge any doors that are locked to us.'

'But the count promised the front door would be unlocked for us.'

'It wasn't the front door I was thinking of. Drakul sleeps in that coffin downstairs. If I get to him again, I mean to end his life, however many centuries he has lived it.'

My plan worked. I began just after dawn, and by mid-morning my charges were ready. I had gauged their power accurately. I returned to our apartment, and with Victoria's help brought a barely conscious Carolyn down to the carriage waiting in the courtyard, just as the count had promised.

Then I went back to the charges I had planted. When the first of them went, they did little more than rock that old castle; but just as I had hoped, I found that the door to the count's sleeping chamber was now blown from its hinges.

Lighting the torches along the way, I descended the stone stairs and found that the door below, like the one above, was off its hinges as well. The coffin was where it had been before, the count sleeping in it.

I looked around frantically for the stake. I had tossed it aside when Carolyn had come down to stop me from destroying Drakul the first time, but now I did not see it. Could Drakul have taken it away?

I turned, and as I did so my foot struck something on the floor. The stake, under my foot. I snatched it up and hurried toward the coffin. But even as I did so, it appeared I was too late. With a groan, Drakul opened his eyes. Impossible, I thought — but of course, here in the castle's basement it was as dark as night — no sunlight reached into this windowless chamber to threaten his well-being.

'You foolish man,' Drakul said with a voice that sounded like the hiss of a serpent. 'Did you really think you could destroy me?'

He started to rise from his coffin, his eyes boring into mine. My legs began to tremble and the wooden stake in my hand grew hot, like burning metal, making me want to drop it. I resisted the impulse. I knew he was only using his wiles to trick me.

I had taken the crucifix with me when I left our rooms, while Victoria kept the Bible with her. With my free hand I frantically searched my pockets for the tiny gold cross. I found it, and snatching it out of my pocket, I held it up before me.

'Get back, you devil,' I ordered. The count cringed before me, and I could feel his power over me waning. At the same time, the cross seemed to give me strength. I raised the stake in my hand — or, rather, my hand seemed to lift itself into the air and aimed the wooden stake at the count like a spear. With a mighty thrust, I sent it into his chest, right where his heart should have been.

For a moment I thought the attempt might have failed. The count stood where he was, blood gushing from the wound. Then, with a mighty groan, he toppled backward into his coffin. As he died, the wolves in the forest outside began to howl, though it was not yet midday. I heard a groan behind me and looked, to see Carolyn.

Carolyn! I had left her with Victoria. They should both have been safely in the carriage outside.

'John,' she said in a hoarse voice, 'give me the cross.'

I thrust it at her. She took it and clasped it to her bosom. Then, with another groan, she sank to the floor.

I went to her, but I did not even have to touch her to know that Carolyn was dead. When I knelt beside her, however, I saw that she was smiling, and I knew that finally she was at peace. I could not bear to leave her there, and I gathered her up in my arms.

When I took one last look at Count Drakul, I saw that the flesh had faded from his body. He was once again only a skeleton with a stake buried amid his ribs.

I carried Carolyn to the carriage. Victoria clambered down when she saw us approach.

'Thank heaven. I don't know how she got out of here without my seeing her go. One minute she was right here, and the next she had disappeared. Is she . . . ?'

I gave my head a shake, and I saw the moment when she understood. 'I couldn't leave her here,' I said.

'No,' she agreed. 'We'll take her with us.' We laid the lifeless Carolyn across the rear seat.

'There's one more thing I must do,' I said. 'I will be back in a moment. Stay here.'

I hurried inside to where I had left my equipment. I had earlier rigged the rest of it to blow, but I had not detonated everything before. Now I set the rest of it to go off in a few minutes' time.

Then I ran back outside, leaped onto the carriage, and gave the reins a snap. As we started to speed away, the dynamite behind us went off, and we looked back to see Castle Drakul come down in a heap of broken stones and great clouds of dust. No one would ever again waken the sleeping count.

'But won't the Romanian government question the explosion?' Victoria asked.

'Explosion?' I repeated in mock innocence. 'You mean the earthquake? The one I had long predicted?'

The sun was almost at its apex. My spirits rose with it. I urged the horse on. We had yet a long and difficult journey ahead of us.

We do hope that you have enjoyed reading this large print book.

Did you know that all of our titles are available for purchase?

We publish a wide range of high quality large print books including:
**Romances, Mysteries, Classics
General Fiction
Non Fiction and Westerns**

Special interest titles available in large print are:
**The Little Oxford Dictionary
Music Book, Song Book
Hymn Book, Service Book**

Also available from us courtesy of Oxford University Press:
**Young Readers' Dictionary
(large print edition)
Young Readers' Thesaurus
(large print edition)**

For further information or a free brochure, please contact us at:
**Ulverscroft Large Print Books Ltd.,
The Green, Bradgate Road, Anstey,
Leicester, LE7 7FU, England.
Tel:** (00 44) **0116 236 4325
Fax:** (00 44) **0116 234 0205**

Other titles in the
Linford Mystery Library:

STING OF DEATH

Shelley Smith

Devoted wife and mother Linda Campion is found dead in her hall, sprawled on the marble floor, clutching a Catholic medallion of Saint Thérèse. An accidental tumble over the banisters? A suicidal plummet? Or is there an even more sinister explanation? As the police investigation begins to unearth family secrets, it becomes clear that all was not well in the household: Linda's husband Edmund — not long home from the war — has disappeared; and one of their guests has recently killed himself . . .

MRS. WATSON AND THE SHAKESPEARE CURSE

Michael Mallory

London, 1906. One of the world's foremost Shakespeare scholars presents a paper at Madame Tussaud's which claims that the real author of the works accredited to the Bard of Avon was none other than Queen Elizabeth I. Few in his audience, including the redoubtable Amelia Watson, wife of Doctor John H., take him seriously — but shortly afterward he is found murdered in his hotel room. Worse — Amelia's actor friend, Harry Benbow, is falsely accused of the crime. Can Amelia clear his name before Scotland Yard catch up to him?

SCREAMWORLD

Edmund Glasby

When the insurance official sent to check out an accident at a gruesome theme park called Screamworld goes missing, private investigator John Brent is called in. Could the disappearance be linked with the unusual creator of the park — or are there other forces at work? What Brent finds behind the park's ghastly façade far exceeds his worst expectations, and threatens to drag him into a terrifying maelstrom of murder and madness, as the true purpose of the main attraction becomes all too clear . . .

BUSH CLAWS

Denis Hughes

On a geological expedition into dark-
est Africa, Rex Brandon encounters
two explorers, Litzgor and Dorton, both
suffering from malaria. Brandon admin-
isters medical aid, and on recovering,
the two men relate a fantastic tale.
Whilst prospecting in an unexplored
region, they had fled when attacked by
a hostile native tribe led by a white
woman with a mighty lion at her side.
Litzgor had dropped his new inven-
tion, an electronic box — now in the
hands of the mystery woman. Brandon
agrees to help, placing his expedition
in terrifying danger . . .